Charm School
Lip Service

LESSON 6

LYNN GARCIA CARMER

Charm School Lip Service: Lesson 6
By Lynn Garcia Carmer
ISBN: 978-1-7364456-7-9
Copyright © 2021, Lynn Garcia Carmer
Print Edition

Cover Design: Kari March
Karimarch.com

Editor: Eliza March
badmamamae.com

Photo
wanderbookclub.com

Formatter: BB eBooks
www.bbebooksthailand.com

Newsletter

Sign up for MY NEWSLETTER for all the latest and greatest!
www.lynncarmerauthor.com

Carmer's Charmers

**Join my super-fun and fabulous, private Facebook group
Carmer's Charmers to talk book boyfriends… and more!**
facebook.com/groups/1850040638552307

Chapter 1

LIP JOB

SATURDAY

WHY CAN'T MY mouth form the word no?

Ren Skala meandered through Ms. Belle's Charm School, taking the longest and slowest path possible. Every light blazed, creating a homey glow highlighting doilies, grandfather clocks, and gleaming hardwood floors. As she headed toward impending doom, she reached inside her oversized bag and grasped her favorite crystal, amethyst, to calm her and reduce negativity.

If I'm honest, the only negative one around here is me.

Ren peeked around the corner and wished this was a nightmare, so she could wake up. Nope. Not a dream. In fact, the place was hopping. A nice-sized crowd milled outside of the old California craftsman. The ballroom was transformed with about twenty square tables scattered around the large room.

This part of the school looked absolutely amazing. Her friends had inherited the mansion and completely modernized it after deciding to teach *adult* classes to keep the place out of foreclosure. The very adult classes were the talk of the town. Ren should know—she'd attended *every single one*.

Tonight, her visit had absolutely nothing to do with naughty techniques. It was so much worse. The charm school had expanded its reach into one of the world's most terrifying endeavors.

Speed dating.

Again, you could have shut this down with one simple no.

Except, that would entail saying the dreaded word to one of her best friends in the world and then having to explain *why* she'd said no. It hurt too much to go into those kinds of details.

"Ren!" Brynn Calvo toddled over, her long bangs framing dark-rimmed glasses that continually slipped down her nose. Brynn carefully hugged Ren, her pregnant belly lost somewhere inside her beige cardigan. "Ready to have some fun?"

"No. Definitely not. I'm not fun. At all. Nope." Ren returned the hug with shaky arms, hoping Brynn would let her slip away without notice.

"Yes, you are! You're super-fun."

"I am not. I'm a walking mood killer."

"You're the most outgoing person I know. A total people-person. Why so shy now?"

"Because I don't date. *Ever.* I can't believe Aitana forced me to be here." She hugged Brynn again because she felt bad about complaining.

"I heard that." Aitana sauntered up to the two of them, a wide grin plastered across her face. She'd been a constant at the charm school, years ago, when they'd all attended as kids. She was also the creator and evil genius that had sweetly manipulated Ren into coming to this *fakakta* event.

"Good. Can I go home?" Ren pleaded and looked around, trying to find a dark corner to hide in. Talking to people was usually her favorite thing to do, but it had been *years* since she dated and was in way over her head.

"I know you're nervous. I would be too, but remember, this is our pilot run. All I need you to do is research. Talk to the guys, help us refine the event. I would appreciate the feedback so, so much." Aitana flashed her pouty face.

"Cut it out. I hate it when you make that face." Ren sighed.

"You're still going to do it though, right?"

"Yes. Of course I am." Because disappointing people wasn't in her DNA.

"*Thank you.* I'm going to go over my introduction one more time, but I'll be at the back of the room if you need me." Aitana kissed her cheek and sauntered away.

"How did you get stuck helping today?" Ren asked Brynn.

Brynn was one of four quadruplets, known around town as the Calvo Quads. They'd inherited the charm school six months past when their mentor, Belle Charles had died. But Brynn was a community college professor and was only superficially involved with the school.

"You look like you might drop. Here, sit down." Ren led Brynn into the ballroom and sat her at one of the tables designated for the speed daters.

"Phew, thanks. This feels good." Brynn laughed and brushed her bangs off her forehead. "I've been on my feet a little more than usual." She rubbed her belly. "As for your question about my sisters, everybody is either out of town or busy. That left me."

"I can't believe everybody's gone. I'm used to there being so many of you." Ren laughed and grabbed a pillow, stuffing it behind Brynn's back to give her lumbar support.

"I know. Thank God for Aitana. This is her show. I haven't had to do anything. Plus, it gave me a place to hang for the night. Alexei took off to meet with a private client in Northern California, so I'm on my own. His lamps are selling well." Brynn's brooding baby daddy was an extraordinary artist, specializing in stained glass lamps.

Ren glanced up at the casement windows lining the back wall, noticing the exquisite detail of the bronzed angel etched in glass. Alexei had surprised Brynn with it last year. "He's so talented."

"He is." Brynn gave Aitana a thumbs-up. "Looks like we'll be starting soon."

Ren itched to make a run for it. The reality of the night ahead set in.

"Hey, are you okay?" Brynn grabbed her hand and smiled.

"I'm trying to hold it together. I really am. But I don't think you understand how insane this is for me. I haven't dated since *high school*," she whispered, grabbing a chair to sit next to her friend. She ran her hand over the starched tablecloth, fighting the urge to white knuckle the rectangular table. "I'm rusty."

"I know exactly what you mean. I'm in front of students all day, but when I had to teach the Sex Toys class here at the school," Brynn leaned in and continued, "I've never been so scared in my life. But if Ms. Belle taught me anything, it was there are times when you have to go for it. Put yourself out there. You never know where it may take you."

Omigosh. "I'm not as brave as you."

"Are you kidding? I'm a wimp. It helped that I had Alexei as my partner." She winked and looked at her watch. "Aitana is signaling me. I better go." Brynn stood a little awkwardly, slowly slipping to the side.

Ren popped up and grabbed her arm. "Careful."

"Thanks. I have a bad ankle, and with all this extra weight, I'm kind of unsteady on my feet." Brynn hugged Ren again and looked toward the wide oak doors leading into the ballroom. "Everybody's heading in. I'll be right back."

"No, wait…" But her willowy friend moved quickly for a woman in her third trimester.

Time had run out. The crowd streamed into the ballroom, searching out their name tags. It took minutes for everyone to settle down.

Speed dating was a completely different vibe from the usual classes. Those were attended by a rowdy crowd ready to have a wild time. Tonight, everybody looked single and alone. There were no woo-hoo girls or bawdy men ready to get down and dirty. They all looked a little like her, scared to death.

Maybe I can *do this.* Think of them as your clients, needing a little extra help. Not potential *lovahs.* She giggled and gave herself a mental high five at the funny, an action she found herself doing more and more because she was home alone most nights.

Taking a deep breath, she walked around the room and found the table with her name tag, small notebook, pen, and the cutest little timer. It all became too real.

I can do this. I can do this… Maybe. She tugged at her wispy lavender wig the tiniest bit, wishing she'd gone for a longer length so she could hide behind the locks. For a split second, she'd almost worn the dark-brown one that looked the most like her natural hair, but it would have been a cop-out. A way to hide. She'd made peace with who she was a long time ago, and there would be no backtracking now.

She'd gone bold and worn her lavender locks.

If someone didn't want to date her because of it, their loss. Not that she would actually date anyone after this. Her life was far too complicated for men, or dating…or toe curling sex.

God, I miss sex.

There was only one man that had ever tempted her to throw caution to the wind, and the last time she'd seen him in the flesh had been right here at the charm school. The Quads had thrown a Christmas auction to raise money for the school, and he'd stomped down a runway in the backyard, scowling and glaring at anyone who looked his way.

He'd looked devastatingly hot.

But even better than his rock-hard body was his super sexy mind. She'd inconspicuously gathered tidbits of information on him and learned he'd skipped a grade. The hottest guy she'd ever met was some sort of math genius.

Someone had paid hundreds to go out on a date with him. The urge to bid had been overwhelming, but Theo Romero was a fantasy she couldn't indulge. No matter how many times he'd given his number to one of the Calvo Quads to pass along to Ren, she didn't dare risk the temptation.

That made everything a thousand times harder. They'd never spoken—only ever stared at each other from afar—but the connection was intense and undeniable. She'd never called, but she'd immediately stored his number in her cell under *Herd*. Short for hot-nerd. Who would ever have guessed that an MMA style fighter with bulging muscles and a major frown would be so smart?

Ding, ding, ding.

"Attention everyone." Aitana tapped a pen against the side of a champagne flute. "We'll be starting in a few minutes. I wanted to remind you that we aren't selling alcohol because the school doesn't have a liquor license, but we do allow you to BYOB or BYOW. None of the hard stuff, please. Especially you, Brynn." Aitana's husky laugh wafted over the crowd, relaxing a few tense faces into smiles. "Buckle up, boys and girls. In five, we're gonna get our dates on!"

Chapter 2

TONGUE TWISTER

GIRD YOUR LOINS, *girlfriend. This is happening.*

Setting down her oversized bag filled with charts and far too much junk, Ren concentrated on her stainless steel wine tumbler, the one that held at least *two* full cups of red gold.

Her first sip did nothing to ease her tension, but it gave her a second to mentally prep for the coming horror. It took a few minutes to look around the room—to study the goods. Aitana had hinted the men would be so attractive that they'd knock her out of her self-imposed celibacy.

Not gonna happen.

They looked presentable enough—an ocean of khaki as far as the eye could see. Very corporate America vibe, even the ones with man buns. Aitana had done a great job of finding employed dudes you could bring home to momma. Not a lot with stacks of muscles like a certain man she knew, and definitely no one with intricate tattoos she wanted to trace with her tongue, but all very nice.

All of this was quite overwhelming for a girl most guys "friend-zoned" within minutes of meeting her. First, they'd swear they'd never felt so comfortable. The next was immediately followed by a request to be set up with a friend. She took a long drag of wine over that depressing thought, sighed, and watched Aitana wend her way back to the front of the room.

Girding. Loins. Now.

"Attention everyone. I think I forgot to thank you earlier. You're truly helping me make my dreams come true." Aitana waved, her corkscrew curls brushing her shoulder blades. Today she wore a blood-orange wrap that emphasized every dangerous curve. "I'm going to explain the rules. But first, does everybody have the app downloaded so you can keep track of who you like?"

A few people murmured *yes* or clapped in confirmation. It seemed like an overwhelming number of shy and reserved people. Ren took another sip, the wine kicking in the tiniest bit as she remembered Aitana had created the One and Done app with introverts in mind.

"Okay, this is a beta run. Tonight's on the house. Even though it's a run through, the app and my services will be readily available very soon." She laughed and took a deep breath. "I'm sorry, I feel like I'm rushing. I'm told I talk too fast." Aitana pointed at the back of the room and cocked a brow.

Ren craned her neck to see who her vivacious friend was pointing out, and giggled. Blue Lagos was there, leaning against the wall with his arms crossed. Of course he'd shown. Blue and Aitana had grown up together. They'd both attended Ms. Belle's Charm School every summer as kids.

"You're doing fine." Blue winked, his deep voice as relaxed as his pose. Nothing ruffled that man. Except maybe Aitana. She was the only one who could get under his skin.

"I know." She winked. "Okay, what am I forgetting? The app! Let's start there. I designed this process to be as user friendly, and nonconfrontational, as possible. The guys will move about and the women are seated with timers set to go off every two minutes. That's right. Only *two minutes*. It allows you just enough time to decide if you're interested—and it leaves no room for awkward silences. If you feel a connection, you log onto the app and click the thumbs-up. That way, no one feels judged or awkward. We only match up people if both have indicated an interest."

This is brilliant. Ren was so excited for her friend and selfishly, for herself. At her best estimation, at two minutes per chat, that meant she could be done within the hour.

Win-win!

"By the way, the next class will be geared toward the LGBTQ community. All information is in the pamphlets in the back." She fanned herself. "Is it hot in here, or am I nervous?"

"*You're* hot." Someone who sounded suspiciously like Blue yelled from the back of the room.

"Not what I meant but it's appreciated nonetheless. I'm so excited. Okay, grab your phones. All the women should be seated at this point." Aitana waved on a few stragglers. "Come on over. You don't have to wait for me to finish speaking. We're all friends." She laughed, a warm rush of sound that always made Ren happy. Everything about Aitana was like that, sheer joy and love. Until you made her mad. Ren had been smart enough never to make that mistake.

"On your mark, get set, go!"

BEEP.

The vino relaxed Ren enough to ease her panic. *I can do this.* She was a people person, and loved to shoot the shit. The key would be to make her situation very clear so none of the guys fell in love.

Ha! Another mental high five on that one.

The more she thought about it, this might be ideal. She'd have a captive audience for two-minute intervals.

Ren flipped open her notebook, reviewing her list of questions. She'd actually spent a good deal of time on them, imagining the scenario was real and all the crucial questions she would want answered. No matter how ridiculous they seemed.

After longer than a few seconds, Ren looked at the seat in front of her. Empty. Yet it looked like all of the other tables were full with their timers audibly ticking down. She sat toward the back of the room, so maybe they had more women than men. No problem. In less than two minutes, she would be chatting with the next Mr. Speed Dater.

BEEP.

Men shuffled to their left and, still, no one sat in front of her. One guy walked past quickly, refusing to meet her eye.

What the heck?

BEEP. BEEP. BEEP.

It happened again and again. Dumbfounded, Ren glanced around and met Blue's eyes. She lifted her hands in a "what's going on?" motion. Blue smiled and shrugged, not concerned in the least. When she made to stand, he shook his head but didn't motion further. Blue had an easy way about him that made people listen. Trusting him enough to hope he knew something she didn't, she sat back down.

A small part of her, an old ugly part, took her back to when she'd first lost her hair. At eighteen, she'd woken up with a clump on her pillow. After years of hair loss and regrowth, she'd been diagnosed with Alopecia Areata. In order to get off the hamster wheel, she'd cut off most of her remaining hair and then marched into a wig shop and bought Margarita, a fall of dark-brown, curly hair that closely matched her own.

It had taken a few years, and countless more wigs, before it became a part of who she was. Her hair varied week by week, sometimes day by day. Whatever mood struck. If people were kind and genuinely interested, she had no problem discussing her autoimmune disease.

But now that it was obvious men were deliberately avoiding her table, she was reminded of the few cruel encounters she'd lived through. The most recent, only a few months back, during a charity volleyball game. Sighing, she shook off the reverie, no longer interested in living in that dark head-space.

Hell, if no one wants to talk to me, I can always get some work done. She stuck her nose into her bag and fumbled around, looking for her latest case file.

"Ren?" The deep rumble of her name skated down her spine, making her shiver.

She froze. Somehow she knew, deep down in her frantically beating heart, that her life would never be the same.

Chapter 3

CUNNING LINGUIST

*H*E'S HERE. IN *front of me. In the flesh.*
The surrounding noise dropped away. Ren no longer perceived the crowded room, the sound of soft chatter, or the beep of the date-swap bell. Instead, she felt sucked into a tunnel and a frowning god greeted her at the end. Her attention was singular, and when this particular kind of reverie hit, she floated in her own musings. Wallowed in the sheer joy and wonder of whatever had caught her interest.

Today it was Theo Romero, aka the Cuban, aka the man of her dreams. Literally.

He didn't disappoint. Ren took her time studying his massive frame. So much better than her fantasies. Tonight, he wore a biker jacket, a long-sleeved camel sweater over dark jeans, and boots.

Theo was a rough-edged MMA fighter who made scowling look extremely hot. *Devastatingly so.* He had dark hair shaved at the sides and longer on top. Thick brows sat over striking hazel eyes. He had the type of gaze that snared you and never let go. His square jaw, covered by a short beard, gave her goose bumps because she imagined the course feel against her sensitive palms. She especially loved his busted nose. It saved him from being too pretty. But his pillow lips? It should be illegal for a man to have such a pouty mouth.

It seemed pretty evident he was an old soul—she was very good at deciphering that kind of thing. His super-sexy and mature energy notwithstanding, he looked to be in his mid-twenties. Perfect age, prefect face, body to die for…

Seconds, maybe hours, passed before Ren slowly came back to reality.

Omigod, how long had she been staring? And come to think of it—why hadn't he spoken? People were always snapping her out of her daydreams. Wasn't that the polite thing to do?

Instead, Theo stood, arms crossed, studying her in even greater detail than she'd done to him. His eyes were like a green flame, dancing along every feature of her face, then down to her neck and chest.

Her nipples puckered in reaction, and she clutched her bag close to her chest. Still, he didn't say anything. Was that because it was her turn to speak?

Oh God. What had he said? Had he asked a question?

"Hi." She smiled and brushed her fingers along the edge of her lavender wig.

He continued to study her, and it hit her. He'd been as lost in thought as she'd been. It gave her great pleasure to say, "Theo?"

His eyes snapped back to hers, and a rueful smile played along his full lips, transforming his frowning face into a thing of beauty. "You know my name?"

"Of course." She felt her smile stretch her lips.

"Can I sit?"

"Yes." She laughed nervously, overwhelmed with meeting him in person. How many times had she wondered what he would sound like, how he would act if they ever met? "That's the whole point of this, right?"

"Right." He glowered again, not looking excited in the least.

"Speed dating."

"I'm glad you sat down. No one has come over yet." She placed her notebook on the table and smiled self-consciously, a little embarrassed she hadn't addressed this sooner. "Listen. I guess this moment is a long time coming."

"It is?" He leaned in and zeroed in on her mouth.

She licked her lip reflexively, watching as his eyes narrowed. His cologne wafted toward her, and she melted. His masculine scent was an earthy combo of leather and oak. "I owe you an apology."

He sat back in the seat and folded his arms.

His brooding demeanor only made him sexier. *Focus, Ren!* "I should've called you and at least thanked you. I'm not sure exactly what happened, but I heard you took care of things with the mean guy at the volleyball game."

"Thor." He looked down, shaking his head. "That fucking moron."

Ren nodded her head. "I appreciated it. I usually don't get upset when guys make comments like that, but anyway…thank you for defending my honor."

"I'd do it again." His voice was rough.

"You would?" She sucked on her bottom lip. *Devastatingly sexy.*

"I am?" He leaned forward. "You think I'm *devastatingly sexy?*"

"Did I say that out loud?" Damn it. But she couldn't regret the look of awe and heat her words engendered.

"Yeah, you did."

"Sorry. You probably think I'm crazy for saying that. I just meant that it was a romantic thing to do." She winced. "Nope. Not romantic. Didn't mean to say that either since we don't know each other. It was *chivalrous.* That's the word I should have used."

"When I heard what he said to you, well… I wasn't too happy about it."

Ren had sloughed off the negativity months ago. Normally, Thor calling her a bald chick wouldn't have even penetrated her carefully built walls. But it had been a particularly hard day. Guys like that were a dime a dozen, and they couldn't hurt her anymore. But she couldn't resist asking, "What happened then?"

"I walked him a few houses down and popped him in the jaw. He went down hard."

"You didn't even say anything to him beforehand?" Ren's jaw dropped, and it took a few beats of her pounding heart to click it shut.

"Nope. He didn't even remember what happened when they found him sprawled out on the neighbor's lawn."

She loved the idea that he'd defended her honor, but it meant he must be a hothead. And reckless. He could have gone to jail because of her. But instead of reprimanding him, she threw back her head and laughed. A few startled people looked over, but Theo only had eyes for her. "Sorry. I'm told my laugh can be a little loud."

"There's nothing wrong with your laugh. I like it."

Fascinating.

"I shouldn't love that you punched out Thor, but I really do. He hadn't only said stuff about me, he was a total jerk. By the way, what kind of name is Thor?"

"Right? I'm thinking he's overcompensating for something." He cocked a brow.

He's funny too. Doubly devastating. "I didn't think…"

BEEP.

"Oh shoot. Was that the timer?"

"I didn't hear anything. You were saying?" Theo leaned in, his elbows resting on the table, pulling his sweater tight against his broad shoulders. The color perfectly accented his bronze skin, deliciously brown and lickable.

Ren got lost in his gaze. "I didn't think of you as a big speed dater."

"Blue had mentioned it, but I don't know much about it."

"It's pretty simple. Aitana is a computer genius, and she came up with a dating app. The guys are supposed to switch tables every two minutes, but it's weird. So far, no one wants to talk to me." She hefted up her bag. "I was going to start doing some work."

"Did it hurt your feelings that no one came over?" He quickly scratched the side of his shaved head and looked around like he wanted to demolish the guys for skipping her table.

"It's no big deal." *Now that you're here.* "This whole process seemed a little strange to me. But I guess it's more of a safe space for introverts. That's never been my problem. Most people want me to *stop* talking."

"Why would they want you to stop talking?" He cracked his knuckles. No man had ever looked sexier as he contemplated violence—all on her behalf.

"Give it some time. You've only been here a few minutes. That reminds me, the timer has to have gone off. I should pay more attention. But I've been having so much fun talking to you."

Theo cleared his throat and zeroed back in on her. "What would you do if one of those guys sat down?"

"I'd ask them some of the questions I wrote down and get to know them. No big deal."

"You're taking this seriously." The comment made him look a bit guarded.

"What? *Me?* No. I don't date." She cleared her throat. "But Aitana needs the feedback, so I wrote down a list of questions I would ask."

"You don't date?" His thick brows snapped together. "Is that why you didn't call me?"

"Yeah, it is." Her quiet words sat between them, but even as she said them, she couldn't stop staring. She soaked him up like her favorite gravy and biscuits, enjoying every minute. Who knew if she'd ever get to spend time with him again? Her words ensured he'd want nothing to do with her.

"I like the way you look at me, Ren." He leaned in. "Is Ren short for something?"

His gruff question made her sit back and shake her head no, even as she gave in and admitted, "Yes."

"Want to tell me what that is?"

"Not really."

He lifted a brow and waited her out.

"Fine." For once, she didn't want to say no. For some reason, she was ready to tell him everything. "But get ready. It's Adrenilda."

"That's… different." He nodded. "Unique. Like you. But I don't think it fits."

His deep voice was a soft rumble, like silk over sandpaper. *So, so sexy.* "Ren. Rena…" His one-sided smile grew. "*Reina.* That fits much better. *Mi Reina.*"

Ren's Spanish was a little weak. She complained to her *tía* about keeping up with it after her mother died, but it hadn't been anyone's fault. Her father didn't speak or understand it, and *tía* only visited every few months.

Reina. This word she knew. Queen. He was calling her his queen.

BEEP.

Time for a date switch. Sadness pressed in on her. It had been fun talking to Theo.

No one approached. Again. *What the hell?* "That was the timer. I think you're supposed to move to the next lady." She gestured to the table to the right.

"I'm good." He didn't budge, just kept staring with his huge arms crossed on the table. "I'm waiting."

"You are?" Why did his direct stare make her thighs clench?

"Your questions." He ruffled his hair which had grown a few inches on top since she'd last seen him, the strands a mix of dark-brown and gold. "Pretend I'm someone you'd want to get to know."

I do. I do. I do. "Okay."

Gone were the scowls and hesitance, and only the cocky Cuban remained.

Why do I love it so much?

"Why do you love what?" he asked with a tilt of his head.

Oh shit. She'd said that out loud too. "Nothing." Okay, she contemplated giving him the safe questions, but why? Let him get a chance to know the real her, and he'd probably hit the ground running.

"Question one." She looked up and couldn't control the smile inching across her face. The best part about her question was the answer didn't matter. It was all about the reaction. "Do you believe in ghosts?"

He threw his head back and laughed. "*Coño*, this is gonna be fun."

Chapter 4

SNACK AT THE Y

PERFECT FACE, PERFECT body, perfect answer... *perfect tongue ring?!*

When she'd dreamed of Theo Romero—and yes, it was always using his full name—she never thought about hardware. Dear Lord, the sexiest man on the planet had a pierced tongue. Heat pooled between her legs at the thought of what that might feel like.

I'm dying to find out.

"Yeah, I do. My *abuela's* farm in Cuba had a haunted barn. All kinds of crazy stuff happened back in the day, and I grew up on stories about it. I'm a believer." He leaned his elbow on the table. "How about you?"

"How about what?" *Aren't we still talking about tongue rings? No, focus Ren.* He'd answered in the absolutely best way possible. Yes or no didn't matter. It was about the laughter, and Theo's had been... everything. It transformed his scowling demeanor into a thing of beauty.

"Ghosts." His soft laughter rolled over her. "I can't think straight when you get that faraway look on your face. I want it to be about me."

It is! But she couldn't respond that way. She couldn't mess with

Theo, and it was time to rein things back in. "Definitely. I believe in ghosts, too."

He grumbled but sat back, reluctantly accepting the change of subject.

She looked down at her list of questions, for once not wanting to expound on her answers. Instead, it was all about Theo and what she could learn about him. To store for use in the future, during long lonely nights.

The rest of her questions were a combination of hard-hitting and silly, her inner geek coming to the fore. "Correct order of Star Wars movies."

He nodded, and she held her breath, wondering if her assumptions were true. Maybe someone this tough and ripped didn't watch television or movies. Maybe he needed to spend precious time cultivating stacks and stacks of muscles.

"I fight with Blue about this all the time. I'm all about chronological order." He narrowed his gaze, obviously understanding the importance of the inquiry.

She shook her head. "Wow, I'm sorry. So, no prize for you, but I'll move on."

He laughed. "There are prizes?"

"Not for you, Theo Romero. That answer could *not* have been more wrong. Sorry." She giggled. "You've travelled to Hogwarts and the Sorting Hat says…"

She held her breath and whispered the word the same time he said, "Gryffindor."

"Most people think Slytherin." But he patted his chest and smirked, owning his Slytherin energy.

"Not me." Had any of her conversations ever been so sexy?

The smile on his face grew. "I know," his gruff voice dropped. "What a surprise." There was a question in his statement that she wasn't ready to explore.

Her whole body flushed, and she hoped ugly red splotches

hadn't stained her fair neck. With any luck, the light was low enough to hide her reaction. But she couldn't help herself. Every word that dripped from his mouth made her react. She was drowning in awareness and pure, unadulterated lust.

"Ren?" He almost groaned her name. Had she been staring again?

She took the coward's way out and rushed to the next question. "Are you more of a 'me' or a 'we' person?"

He scratched the side of his head. "What do you mean?"

"Do you like doing most things alone or with someone else?" She raised her brows. "Like in school, were you all over the group projects, or would you rather go it alone?" She held her breath on this one. This question was one of her fundamentals. Her ex had always been a loner, going off impulsively by himself and she swore she would find a 'we' one day.

Until plans changed.

He looked away; the fire in his eyes dampened for some reason. "It's just me."

Her mind spun on that answer. He looked sad, but maybe she was projecting. When she had more time, she would dissect every word. For now, she needed to gather more info. "Biggest misconception about you?"

"That I'm a dumb fighter."

Ren gnawed on her thumbnail, until she reminded herself she was supposed to have outgrown that bad habit. "I heard you never lost a match."

"You want to know why?" He ran his gaze right over the spot she'd been biting her nail. "Because I'm the smartest one in the ring, and when I want something, I don't stop until it's mine."

"Oh, my God," she whispered. *That's so hot.* Ren took a gulp of her wine, drowning in endorphins. His intensity, it bled through him. She felt hyper-sensitive to his every word, and a little vulnerable because of it. There was no way he could be as affected as she.

In order to change the mood, so she could *calm down*, she asked, "*RuPaul's Drag Race*? Yay or nay?"

"Never seen it."

"But would you be willing to?"

"With you? Anytime." His leg tapped an incessant beat, as if energy coursed through him, needing a constant outlet. "My *tío* does drag. He's pretty amazing. We should go to a show this weekend." His hazel gaze beamed at her in challenge.

She looked down, shaking her head. Not ready for reality to set in. They'd gotten lucky that no one had interrupted them, but how much longer would she have with Theo Romero, the sex-god that smelled like sin? "I'm sorry. I can't."

BEEP.

Her head snapped up at the sound, the silence between them allowing her to hear the buzzer. She was even more surprised when a guy finally approached the table. "Time's up, my friend."

Saved by the beep. Although she was deeply disappointed. But it might be for the best, considering she'd turned him down. For months, she'd avoided Theo like the plague, and now she couldn't get enough.

"Go away." Theo crossed his arms and stared the man-bunned dater down.

"What?" The guy took a step back when he glanced at Theo's face.

"Leave." The grumpy fighter was back.

"I…"

"*Now.*" Theo cracked his knuckles.

Ren watched with wide eyes as the guy hurried away. She cocked her head to the side and assessed his behavior, starting to get really suspicious. "That wasn't very nice."

"I'm not nice." But he didn't meet her avid gaze.

"Never?" Why did his possessiveness make her happy? "I don't believe that."

"Not to him." Theo tracked him with his intense eyes until he focused back in on her. "Always to you."

"What's going on? Why—"

Another khaki king approached. Theo huffed and looked over his shoulder. "Blue! A little help here. That's two I'm having to deal with."

Two?

Blue pulled himself away from chatting with Aitana, his gait as unhurried as ever. "Sorry. Got tied up. Won't happen again." He winked at Ren and escorted the guy away.

"Happen again?" Realization dawned on her. Although, she probably would have figured it out a lot sooner if she hadn't been distracted by the demanding fighter in front of her. "Did you have Blue make sure no one would speed date me?" Her word choice was poor, but the guilty yet challenging look sported by the Cuban made her think he knew what she meant. "Did you?"

"Yes."

"Theo!"

"I'm shooting my shot." He gripped the edges of the table and sucked her into his presence, his energy. For those few seconds, there was no one else in the room. "All I wanted was a little time."

"Time for what?"

"To see if all of these thoughts, these *feelings* I had for you were insane. We've never spoken, yet I couldn't get you off my mind. None of this makes sense. I see you and you ignore me for months. I wanted to prove to myself that you couldn't live up to my fantasies."

Her response got caught in her throat. She curled her hands to stop herself from touching him. She had a real problem with touch. A problem because she craved it, and anytime she was around someone she liked, she wanted it. It grounded her, connected her to whomever she interacted with. It was her absolute favorite part of getting to know someone.

"Ask me. Ask me if you live up to my expectations. Ask me if what I feel is real."

She gasped, transfixed by every tiny detail. The tic in his jaw, the width of his broad shoulders, and the flash of vulnerability in his intense eyes. She had no right to ask, but she found herself whispering. "D-did I?"

"You exceeded every single one. I see the way you look at me and it..." He rubbed his chest. "I feel it right here. I know this is something real."

Oh my God, that was the most intense thing she'd ever heard after a twenty-minute conversation. But she felt it, too.

"Reina, listen. Go out with me. Give me a chance. I know I look all busted up—"

"You do not!"

"I don't?" He ran a hand over his jaw and smiled—a softer more genuine one than before. So far, he'd shown her an open-mouthed laugh and his playful grin, but this was full of surprise and sincerity. "Why have you ignored me? Why won't you give us a try?"

"That's a long story."

"Damn. You're killing me," he mumbled to himself, and the flippant words stuck in her throat. Maybe he wasn't as cocky as he seemed. Then he zeroed in on her lips and said, "The way I see it, you owe me, Reina. Remember?" He threw her words back at her. "My knuckles were sore for days after I knocked Thor out."

"They were?" And there it was. Her in. She couldn't help herself. She grabbed his hand and ran her fingers over his callused palm. Delicious. This man worked, and worked hard. She knew he was a fighter. She flipped his hand over and traced every knuckle. They did look bruised. "Really?"

"No. I lied. I wanted—" He groaned. "The way you touch me." His deep voice rumbled through her, tickling all the most delicious spots.

Every part of her was attuned to him, and the feelings were intense. "I had one more question I forgot to ask," Ren said, looking at his full lips. Men shouldn't have such tempting lips.

"Ask me."

"Wanna make out to ease the tension?" She felt the smile grow on her face.

"*Jesus*, woman. Come here." He half stood to pull her across the table—

"*Hello!* PDA much? How embarrassing."

Ren blinked, only inches from Theo's warm skin. Tearing herself out of his sensual gaze, she saw a statuesque redhead standing over them. She was absolutely stunning and looked vaguely familiar.

"This is the worst date ever. Everybody's so old."

Date… wait, *date?* "You took a date to speed dating?" Ren tried to tug her hand out of his, but he held on tight.

"No." Theo scowled and looked at the young redhead. "Get out of here, Viviana."

"Yes." She stared at Ren. "I bid on him and won at the auction."

Theo let go of Ren's hand, brushing his thumbs against her as if even his fingers were reluctant to let go. "That was months ago. At the Christmas Auction, and I fulfilled that agreement."

"That didn't count. You took me out on a group date."

"You're like twelve. I wasn't going alone." He growled. "I only brought her here to even out the numbers. I didn't want to mess up Aitana's equation."

"You and your stupid math. And I'm eighteen!" She stomped her foot, ruining any hope of looking mature.

Ren couldn't process what was happening. The whole thing was confusing and Theo looked annoyed. So Ren dropped into super-friendly mode. Her annoying default. "Hi. I'm Ren."

"Viviana." She flicked her hair over her shoulder. "Why were the two of you touching like that? In public? I'm bored." She whipped out her phone. "I'm totally going on Instagram Live to say this place sucks ass."

What? "Wait." *Approach her with kindness.* It was Ren's motto and usually helped when she had to navigate difficult situations at the hospital. No matter how much she wanted to smash someone in the face—she'd make nice for Aitana's dream. Her fledgling app didn't need any bad publicity, and Ren had a sinking feeling this beauty probably had a lot of followers. "Hey, hi. I'm so sorry. Theo said he'd gotten hurt, and I was checking his hand. Right, Theo?"

"No. I was holding your hand because I wanted to." The frown grew with each word.

"But you wouldn't want Aitana to get any bad publicity." She cocked her head toward Viviana, who had her face in her purple phone.

Theo didn't bother to look away from Ren. "Viviana, put your phone away. No one's going live. We aren't on a date. You're supposed to find a date *here*. Someone else. Besides me." A muscle ticked in his jaw.

"You were totally about to 'do it.'"

"What? No. I was checking his hand, remember? See, look at the bruises." Ren pointed at his knuckles, uncomfortable with the whole situation. Why did she have to explain any of this? Why had she even held his hand?

"Lemme see," Viviana demanded.

When Theo refused to show her his hand, Ren pleaded with him with her eyes. He sighed and stuck his hand in front of her face.

"Holding hands is not the same as *doing it*." Theo curled his palm before Viviana touched him and stepped toward Ren. "We work together. She's like a little sister."

"I'm a grown-ass woman now. So there." Her strong statement lost steam by the time she said the last sentence.

BEEP. BEEP. BEEP

"That's the signal folks." Aitana called from the front of the ballroom. "That's the end of your evening. The app should immediately notify you of your matches. Don't forget to let me know if there are any glitches. I'm counting on your help to make this business venture work. Good night and drive safely."

"Okay, well…" Ren seized the moment with mixed emotions— grateful for Viviana's interruption, and not. It was a reminder she had no right to ask Theo personal questions or hold his hand. No matter how much her fingers itched to touch him again. "I'm going to get going. Thanks for the help, Theo. I'll report back all the findings to Aitana. Nice to meet you, Viviana."

The young girl with flawless makeup and legs for days waved an absent hand in her direction, which apparently meant crisis averted?

She took a few steps back.

"Reina, don't go. Wait."

The heat in his words made her stomach flutter. Almost half-way to the door, she made a beeline for the exit. She'd explain everything to Aitana and Brynn on her drive home. Unable to resist, she took one last look back. "I have to go. I'm sorry."

Theo completely ignored Viviana and took a step toward her.

Ren made it out to her car in record time, crushing any spark they'd had between them. Even though it had been the right thing to do, she felt the loss down to the depths of her soul.

Chapter 5

CLEANING THE CARPET

SUNDAY

*B*ACK AT THE *scene of the crime.*

Ren tapped at the backdoor, breathing in the jasmine surrounding the sides of the school. She hardly registered the hydrangeas that usually brought her so much joy, the blues and pinks, her absolute favorite flowers. Now her association with the school involved a sexy Cuban and defective speed dating.

"Ren. Thank you again for doing this. You're a lifesaver." Brynn hugged her tight. "I was going to ask you to spend the night yesterday, but you took off right after speed dating." Brynn's far too discerning gaze studied her reaction.

Not going there. "You know I'd do anything for you." Ren had agreed weeks ago to help cull some of Ms. Belle's old paperwork.

"Hand me your bag, and I'll set it down in the room."

"Don't you dare. No lifting in your condition."

Brynn laughed. "I'm fine." She pointed at the table in the foyer. "You can set your stuff down there."

"How many weeks are you?"

"Twenty-three weeks."

"Let's go back to Ms. Belle's study. That's where all of her paperwork is." Brynn pushed her dark-rimmed glasses up her nose. "You sure you're up for this? There's a lot of stuff to wade through."

"I'll do my best." This was the part of the school that still held Ms. Belle's stamp. Ren studied an intricate cuckoo clock as they made their way toward the former owner's study. She'd owned and operated the place for close to fifty years. "I'll probably only be familiar with the medical stuff."

The Calvo Quads had inherited the school six months prior, but they were only now going through their mentor's paperwork.

"Since you're a social worker, I figured you could help us. Especially because you work at the hospital." Brynn sat behind the shabby chic desk dominating the room. "Look at our new sign for the upcoming class."

Ren leaned over her shoulder and read it out loud, "Lip Service. This One's for the Ladies." She looked at Brynn. "That's awesome!"

"Yay. I think so, too."

"Are you freaked out that there'll be a lot more guys attending this class?" Ren fanned herself, overheating *for* her friend.

"Yes! All of the other classes were techniques geared toward men. This class is a switcheroo. It's about going *downtown* on the girly bits." Brynn's husky laughter was contagious. She was a sucker for inappropriateness and bad words; they always made her giggle.

"I give you all the props. I'd die if I had to teach that class." Ren ran her gaze over the neatly stacked file folders, all labeled with different medical conditions and years. It always felt so invasive to handle such personal items, especially medical information. "Not that I have much experience with the topic of dating in general."

Brynn's hazel green gaze narrowed in on her own.

Uh-oh, she'd broken one of her own rules—never mention anything about her love life because it invited questions about her *love life.* Or lack thereof.

"And why is that?" Brynn folded up the sign and tucked it under the desk.

"Why is what?" Ren became fixated on removing invisible pieces of lint off her polka dotted dress.

"You know what. A perfectly gorgeous man, a bit grumpy but still gorgeous man, couldn't take his eyes off you last night."

"I have no idea who you're talking about." Ren winced, realizing she better up her game if she wanted to throw Brynn off track. She wasn't ready to talk about men, or dating, or one particular hot-nerd, she may or may not be secretly obsessed with.

"You know I'm talking about Theo. Remember him? The guy who literally scared away the other daters so he could talk to you."

Oh, I remember. Those intense hazel eyes, the curled lip, the way he dismissed everyone around him. Yet he'd shown interest in her. It'd made her feel special. "That was a misunderstanding, I guess?"

"You asking or telling?"

"I…"

"I'm sorry. I shouldn't be pushing you. It's just… Theo's had it rough. I thought maybe you saw beyond his tough exterior."

"What do you mean?" Ren was utterly captivated and immediately wanted to know every detail. She shouldn't ask, but she couldn't help herself.

"Never mind. You're not interested, right? I'll keep all that info to myself." Brynn cocked a brow and waited.

"But…" No, she resisted taking the bait. No matter how amazing, and devastatingly sexy he was, he was off-limits. "Okay."

"Boo."

"Brynn, stop." Ren laughed.

"Fine. Let's get to work." Brynn groaned and stood, looking lovely in an oversized sweater and white jeans. "This is the first box of paperwork. I'll have you start with it while I go through the old filing cabinet." She pointed at a box on the desk. "Here, let me—"

"No, I've got it." Ren jumped up to grab the container.

"Don't be silly. It's big but only half full. I'm the one who put it on the desk to begin with." She grabbed the indented handles and lifted it easily. "See. Light. It's kind of awkward to navigate." She came around the desk and walked toward Ren.

"Brynn, wait. Let me—"

Before Ren could react, Brynn tipped to the side, going down hard on her hip. The box of paperwork flew through the air.

"Oh God, Brynn. Are you okay?" Ren dropped to her knees and pushed the box out of the way.

"I'm sorry." Brynn winced. "It's my stupid ankle again."

"It's okay. You're going to be fine."

"Ren. I went down hard." She cupped her belly. "What if the baby—"

"No, no, no. No jumping to conclusions." Ren snapped into professional mode, comforting Brynn like she would any one of her patients. "Tell me exactly how you feel. What hurts?"

"My ankle burns like a motherfucker."

Ren barked out a nervous laugh. *Brynn, cursing?* Had she gone delirious from pain?

Brynn laughed softly. "I couldn't resist. I never curse because I laugh so much, but the pain is pretty much solving that problem."

"Where does it hurt besides your ankle?"

"My hip." She slowly sat up and reached for the glasses that had fallen off her nose. "And there's some tightness in my belly."

Shit. "Okay, no problem. But just in case, I think that the best idea would be to call—"

"No! You're going to say Alexei, right? You *cannot* call him. He's out of town and he'll freak, absolutely go mental if he knows I hurt myself."

"You got it." Of course Ren wouldn't call Brynn's moody baby daddy. The one who loved her with a borderline obsession. "As of this moment, he's dead to me. I'll never call him again. Not that I ever have…" She brushed the bangs out of Brynn's eyes. "I was actually going to recommend your ob-gyn. You know, the trained professional who handles stuff like this for a living." Ren smiled to lessen the sarcasm.

"It's Sunday afternoon. They're closed."

I have her right where I want her. "That's true." She rubbed her back. "Perfect. We'll head straight to the hospital then."

"*What?* I don't want to go to the hospital."

Ren didn't have to ask why. She understood that if Brynn allowed herself to go, then she'd have to admit how serious the situation was. She'd seen many an injured patient fight admittance. "You have to talk to a professional. To make sure you're okay. So you either call the doc or go to the ER."

"Okay, okay, you're right."

"Let's start simple. How about I get your phone, and we'll leave a message for the answering service at the doctor's office? I'm sure a nurse or the doctor herself will give us a call."

"Can I get up?"

Hell no. "Why don't you stay put until they give us the all clear. Just in case."

Brynn swiped the phone, and while she was searching her contacts, the phone rang. "Holy shit. It's Alexei!" She tossed the phone at Ren.

"Why are you giving it to me? He's *your* psycho boyfriend." Ren juggled the phone like a hot potato.

"Because this is your fault."

"Me? What did I do?"

"You said I didn't have to talk to Alexei!"

"I didn't know he'd call."

"I know. It's all my fault." Brynn squeezed Ren's hand in a death grip. "But if I talk to him, he'll make me go to the hospital. Fix this. Please."

Ren wasn't used to seeing this side of her unflappable friend.

She must be really scared. "Okay, okay. I've got this. No problem."

The last time she'd gone toe to toe with Alexei had been at White Memorial Hospital and he'd been the worst patient to deal with, refusing to communicate with anyone but Brynn, insisting every day he was well enough to leave even though he'd suffered extreme injuries. "Hello?"

"Who's this?"

"Hey, Alexei, it's Ren."

"Where's Brynn?" As usual, no small talk.

"She's right here, but we have a bit of a situation." She took a deep breath. "I'm going to ask you to remain calm and let me ex—"

"Where the hell is Brynn?! What happened? Ren, I swear to God..."

"She tripped, but—"

"Is she okay?" His voice dropped to a hoarse whisper. The fear in the deep timbre touched her. "Listen to me, Alexei. She's going to be fine. It was a small tumble, on the carpet in Belle's office. She's sitting up, talking."

"Why isn't she talking to me?"

"Because she doesn't want you to lose your shit. Makes sense, right? And we don't want to scare her because she's already a little worried. We were about to call her doctor and leave a message." She tried to maintain a carefree tone, trying to bring Alexei around to her side in convincing Brynn everything would be fine.

"I would never scare her." His softly spoken words were followed by a harsh command. "Get her to the hospital."

Ren gave her fake laugh and turned away from Brynn. "I'm trying, but she doesn't want to go," she hissed.

"Too bad." He sucked in a breath. "I know what to do. Stay right there. I'll handle it."

"But—"

"Don't. Move. It'll be taken care of. I promise. *Fuck*. I knew I shouldn't have left."

"What are you going to—"

"Promise me you won't leave. I'll take care of everything." He hung up.

"Good news. Alexei is totally calm. Totally." Please don't let me get struck down for blatantly lying to her friend. She turned back to Brynn. "He's taking care of everything. We just need to stay put."

"Damn it! What is he cooking up? Can you get me a pillow?" Brynn groaned. "It's not worth fighting him when he's like this."

Ren made Brynn as comfortable as possible. "I have to ask. Do you feel like there's been any bleeding or discharge—anything out of the ordinary?"

"I don't know." Brynn's eyes went wide behind her glasses. "You won't let me get up to go check," she whispered. "But it doesn't feel like it. I am having some Braxton Hicks though."

Ren was familiar with the tightening of the uterus some women felt before labor. "Have you had them before?"

"Yes."

"See. So it may not even be because of the fall." *Please, please let that be true.* "Everything's going to be okay."

Brynn took a few deep breaths and closed her eyes. "I think so, too. With the fall and now Alexei freaking out, my heart is racing a bit."

"Totally understandable. Let me know what I can do to help."

"You can sit with me and hold my hand."

"Perfect! About seventy percent of my job is hand holding, so I'm a professional."

"Not with the Cuban." Brynn peeked open one eye.

"Don't you start with me about him," Ren grumbled and reached for her purse. "I have just the thing that will make you feel better." She pulled out her bag of crystals. "This is Selenite." She sat on the floor and placed the crystal in Brynn's hand. "Do you want me to tell you about its healing properties? Are you comfortable with crystals?"

"I'm comfortable with anything that will help me and this baby." Brynn clutched the stone to her chest.

"Good. Because everything's going to be okay. I promise."

"You know what? I believe you."

"I know. It's my superpower. People believe what I say. I don't know why. Except, of course, in this case because I'm totally telling the truth."

"And you use it to your advantage."

"Shamelessly." They laughed.

Chapter 6

MOUSTACHE RIDE

T HEO REVVED THE engine, ready to do some damage, something that would get his mind off the best fucking night of his
life. An evening that ended in disaster. He could blame Viviana.
Which he did, for most of the drive home, but he understood it was
more than her fault.

Ren had been hesitant from the beginning, continually saying
she didn't want to date anyone while staring at him like he was an
ice cream cone she wanted to devour. He'd never experienced
anything like it.

Theo wanted more.

He revved the Ducati harder, clicking the headset in his helmet
so he could speak to his partner in crime. The same guy that was
dragging his ass, probably hooking up with the latest hunnie. When
it came to women, Blue was a dog.

"We doing this or what?"

Blue took his time putting on his helmet, making sure all his
stuff was strapped down on his Yamaha and eventually answered,
"You got somewhere else to be?"

I wish. But Blue didn't need to know that. Theo tapped the side
of his helmet, enabling communication between him and Blue as

they rode. "Maybe." He revved the bike one last time and said, "*Dale! Vamonos.*"

They took off, racing out of the Warehouse District, weaving in and out of the heavy traffic that seemed a permanent part of California living.

"We going to pretend last night didn't happen?" Blue flew ahead of him, as they headed toward Mt. Wilson, their favorite place to race in the hills.

Theo groaned, not ready to talk about any of it. But patient Blue, his total opposite, would wait him out till he fessed up. Better to get it over with. "That was my plan."

"I like Ren. And I have to tell you. She looked like she was into you. What did you do to fuck it up?"

"That's what I'm trying to figure out. I must have done something." He wove in and out of traffic, probably not the smartest move during rush hour. But this was his release.

"I can't believe she was interested in your grumpy ass, but she was."

"I thought so too."

"Was she upset about Viviana?"

"She didn't help, put it that way. But Ren was pulling back most of the time. There's a story there. I have to find a way to get her to open up."

"Man. I hate to say it."

But he's gonna say it.

"You've been trying with her for six months. That's a lifetime for you. Is there a possibility…"

Don't say it.

"That she's not into you? It happens." He laughed, low and dark. "Not to me. But it happens."

What if Blue's right? "Please, you haven't had a girlfriend in years." Theo revved the bike and took off. "All your one night hook ups are bullshit, and you know it."

"Exactly. Because I don't want a relationship. And I make it abundantly clear to the ladies ahead of time. I'm not a dog, but my relationships don't have much of a shelf life. They expire quickly."

Time to play a little dirty. His favorite way to engage. "I wonder if you'd be saying that if Aitana were single."

Blue pulled ahead and didn't respond for a long time, which was the closest Theo would get to riling him. Blue was cool as ice. His brothers, Tommy and Dare, mentioned stories about him exploding as a kid, but that was a long time ago. Finally chiming in, Blue said, "You're an asshole, you know that?"

"True." But no mention of Aitana. *Score.* He'd hit the target, but instantly regretted it. He hoped his friend didn't feel as dejected as he did. "Now you know how I feel."

"I was trying to look out for you. Damn."

"I'm good."

"But—"

Theo's phone rang, blaring the song from the Japanese Anime, *Attack on Titan.* Thank God. This fool was about to tread on sensitive territory. He held up a hand to Blue and flicked a button on his Bluetooth helmet.

"Theo." Alexei's voice came through the headset.

"*Que bola,* baby. I'm riding with Blue."

"I need your help." Alexei, normally unruffled, never gave a shit about anyone except his *abuela* and his girl. Right now, he sounded panicked. "Now."

"Anything." Familiar tension stole over Theo, his whole system bracing for the bad news. "What do you need?" He motioned for Blue, and they pulled into a convenience store parking lot.

"Brynn needs help. How far are you from home?"

"Five minutes tops."

"Thank fuck." Alexei breathed. "Grab the van and then get to the charm school ASAP. Brynn is going to argue, but you have to take her to the hospital. Understand?"

"The hospital?" Theo couldn't take in enough air. His throat tightened as if caught in a vice grip. *The hospital?* The one place on the face of the planet he never wanted to see again. Even if his leg was shot off, he never planned to step foot in a hospital again.

"Theo, can you do this? I know you hate hospitals, but you're the only one I can trust with this. I need her to be okay…" He paused, the words obviously caught in his throat. "Can I count on you?"

Blue parked next to Theo and pulled off his helmet. "Everything okay?"

Theo shook his head and snapped the hell out of it. "I got this. I'm leaving now. Call me back in five when I'm in the car and let me know the details." He hung up and looked at Blue. "I'm headed to the charm school. Brynn's in trouble. I'll call as soon as I know anything."

"*Shit.* I better call Aitana. She's going to lose her mind." Blue shoved his helmet back on. "Keep me updated. You headed to Huntington Hospital or White Memorial?"

"I'm not sure. I'll call after I get there." He revved the bike, not looking back, concentrating on one task at a time. Get the van. Pick up, Brynn. Don't think about the hospital. Help my best friend's girl. He prayed, said twenty Hail Mary's, any prayer he could think of—*anything* to keep his friend from going through what he had.

Please don't let him lose Brynn.

Chapter 7

BREAKFAST OF CHAMPIONS

R EN PACED WHILE Brynn spoke with the on-call nurse when four ominous notes rang through the school. That meant someone was at the front door. The sound of that doorbell always gave her the creeps.

"Oh God." Brynn swiped her phone and looked at Ren. "The nurse said the same thing you did. She wants me to go to the hospital, just in case."

"Give me a minute to answer the door, and we'll head out."

"But Alexei said we should stay put."

This visitor better have something to do with Alexei or else she'd launch into plan B. Ren rushed down the long corridor, winding her way to the front of the school and passing the infamous ballroom. All the tables had been removed and scattered throw rugs and plush loveseats remained.

"Coming!" Ren swung open the heavy door, and her eyes were blinded by masculine beauty. Theo Romero in gray sweats, a tight sweatshirt, and his biker jacket. "Theo," she breathed, shocked to see him in the flesh again. So soon. She'd barely recovered from the night before.

Who am I kidding? I'll never recover from our time together.

"Reina?" His wide eyes narrowed, and he stalked toward her, no longer the hesitant speed dater from the night before. He grasped the top of the doorframe and leaned in. "Why did you run?"

She guessed it was meant to intimidate, but it only made her melt. He was so intense, and she took a few seconds to enjoy his huge arms and defined shoulders. She wanted to run her hands down his chest and stomach, her fingers itching to touch him even as her mind said, *Snap out of it. This is about Brynn.* "I didn't run."

She left him at the door as she hurried back to Brynn.

He followed right behind her. "The hell you didn't. I finally got to touch you and then you were gone."

Maybe he should cry to Viviana about it. *Gah.* This was another reminder about why she shouldn't involve herself with Theo. Even though it was pretty obvious he wasn't into Viviana, she couldn't help being salty about her. And she had no right to be.

"Reina." He cut her off and slapped a big palm on Brynn's door before she could sneak by. "That was my best first date ever."

For me too, she sighed to herself. Ren opened her mouth to respond, and she heard a whimper on the other side of the door. Pushing his hand out of the way, she whispered, "We'll talk about it later. Right now, we have to help Brynn."

"Shit. You're right." He ruffled his hair. "Sometimes I get a one track mind. What happened exactly? Alexei was light on details."

"She has a bad ankle and went down hard. She says her foot and her hip really hurt." She looked at him to see if he could handle the information. She had never seen him so tense—and he was already a tense person. But he looked resolved, so she continued, "She's also having some minor contractions. We need to get her to the ER ASAP."

"*Carajo.*" He stood stunned for a second before squaring his shoulder and saying, "Tell me what you need me to do." ·

Ren appreciated that he waited for her guidance instead of storming in and trying to take over. He looked like he was ready for battle. She'd peeled back another layer to the onion named Theo Romero. "The most important thing is to stay calm. For Brynn. We're going to take her to the hospital."

His entire body tensed, but he nodded. "I brought the van. We're good."

Once Brynn accepted that the hospital was the best place for her and the baby, it didn't take much convincing to let Theo carry her to his van.

THEO GRIPPED THE wheel, glancing in the rearview mirror every few seconds to check on Reina and Brynn. He'd borrowed the family van, and Brynn was laid out with her head in Reina's lap. Ren kept up a steady stream of chatter—nothing serious and all of it a distraction. Brynn looked like she was doing her best to play along, but she kept grabbing her belly and wincing every few minutes.

All he could do was concentrate on the road and pray.

They careened down the road toward White Memorial. There were closer hospitals, but Reina insisted he drive there so she could take care of Brynn at her place of work.

Coño. He felt so bad for Alexei and Brynn, but his mind kept straying to Reina...to her touch, her outrageous questions, to anything besides hospitals.

I look like shit. He pulled at his shirt, still feeling the cool sweat drying on his back. He probably smelled too. He and Blue had sparred before the bike ride. When Alexei called and said Brynn had fallen, there'd been no time to go home and shower. He's grabbed the family van and raced over.

Thank God Reina had been there.

He didn't know what to do with an injured pregnant lady. His best friend's girl. If anything happened to her, he didn't think Alexei would make it. Since they were kids, Alexei felt things deeper than most, experienced more loss, and he'd finally clawed his way out of the gutter. Brynn was the best thing that ever happened to Alexei, and Theo would do anything to save his friend that pain.

"Theo, you have a lot of math books back here. Why don't you tell us a little about your field of study?" Ren picked up a heavy textbook, *Random Matrix Theory*. She looked like she needed a little help with the mindless chitchat.

"Yeah, I've been interested in RMT and how it relates to Theoretical Physics. Just a little something I've been working on. No big deal."

Ren laughed softly. "Sounds like a big deal to me. I didn't understand most of what you said."

"I've always loved mathematics. This kind of takes it to the next level. Like Modern Mathematics. I've also considered String Theory, but that's a whole separate study." Theo took a quick turn and glanced in the rearview mirror. "I became so obsessed in high school that I worked every day after school with my math teacher. I skipped a grade because of it."

"Wow." Brynn rubbed her belly. "That's impressive. Alexei said you were thinking about reapplying to USC. That's our alma mater."

Theo tensed, not ready to discuss it. He'd already reapplied but didn't want the humiliation of everyone knowing if he didn't get in. Acceptance had come easy right after high school, but his life had imploded after graduation—and he'd bailed at the last minute. USC was probably done with him, but there was no Plan B. Reapplying had been a no brainer, even if the wait made him queasy.

"Make a left here." Ren's husky voice washed over him.

He fought not to stare too long, because he'd crash the damn car and she'd think he was a creeper. But he couldn't resist another peek at her once he paused at a stop sign. God, she was gorgeous. She was a tiny thing with endless curves. He loved everything about her quirky style, lots of scarves and colorful wigs, but it was what lay underneath that kept him up at night. That sexy little body. He'd dreamed about tonguing her beautiful breasts. Full round perfection that he needed to worship. Soon.

Someone honked behind him, and he glared through the rear-view mirror. He had precious cargo—he wouldn't be rushed. Theo followed Ren's directions, enjoying the sound of her sweet voice.

The first time he saw her, he'd been knocked out by her beauty. But it only took seconds to realize the core of who she was had snared him. It made him dangerously preoccupied. He'd taken a blow to the head one too many times because he couldn't stop thinking about her.

Alexei had nothing but praise for Reina. She'd helped to navigate the mine field of paperwork when Alexei's *abuela* had landed in the hospital. Then when Alexei had ended up there, as well. It was high praise from a moody bastard who never had anything nice to say about anybody except Brynn.

From the moment Theo laid eyes on Ren, he'd wanted to know more.

"Park over here." Reina snapped into professional mode as he slowed the car down. "Okay, Theo, while you carry her in, I'll run ahead and get her a room."

"He doesn't need to carry me again. I've got it." Brynn sat up slowly.

"We know that, and yes he does." Ren smiled, in total control.

Total turn on.

She added, "At least until I get you a wheelchair."

Reina leaned closer to Theo, and he froze, waiting to see what she'd do. "Ignore everything she says. Don't put her down until we get her a room, okay?" She brushed her soft hand against his forearm.

He nodded, still feeling the warmth of her touch. He opened the back door and leaned into the back seat. "I'm following orders."

"I know." Tears filled Brynn's eyes. "I feel so stupid. I have a bad ankle, that's all."

Theo's mouth opened and closed like a guppy. He had no idea what to do. They'd never really spoken one-on-one. She was his best friend's girl. They didn't chat much.

I don't do small talk.

But she looked so scared. To ease her panic, he decided to open up, hoping that would make her feel better. He crouched down on the curb next to her. "I'm a little worried too." He cleared his throat.

Brynn wiped her eyes behind her glasses. "Because you like Ren so much, but you think you blew it because you keep frowning at her?"

"No." *Damn it.* He did not frown that much. At least, not at his queen.

"Because you have a bum ankle too, and you're six months pregnant and the world is treating you like an invalid?" Brynn smiled slightly.

Theo chuckled, realizing she was teasing him, maybe getting a little even for everybody bossing her around. It made him like her even more. Brynn had some spice. Good. She'd need it to handle his boy.

"Nah. My ankles are good, but I hate hospitals."

Her gaze zeroed in on him. "I heard you've gone through some tough times."

Alexei must have told her. "They remind me of death. I hate the smell, the feel, it makes my skin crawl."

"But you're still willing to carry me in there, even though you hate it?"

He gave a curt nod.

"Well, then I can be brave enough to let you. It's not about me anymore, is it?" She palmed her belly. "When you talk to Alexei, please tell him not to come home early."

"I promise." Theo gently lifted her out of the van. "As soon as that's what the doctor says. But Reina says you're going to be fine and I believe her."

"You call her Reina?" She winced as he lifted her up. "That's so sweet. I like that nickname. It fits."

"That's why I gave it to her."

"Right." She rolled her eyes. "You're so bossy. But I think she likes that about you. She's the best, Theo. Don't mess this up."

"I can't make any promises." He kicked the door shut with his foot.

"She always knows the right thing to say. And so convincingly. She says it's her super power." Brynn hooked an arm over his shoulders. "How long have you liked her?"

"Months." He carefully walked through the parking lot and made it through the automatic doors of the ER. He tensed when he caught the first whiff of antiseptic, or illness, or whatever the hell caused that awful smell. It made him shudder.

"Want me to keep talking about Ren to keep your mind off things?"

"Hell yeah." His attention immediately swung away from the odor and back to Brynn.

"Well, she's super smart and kind. I think she has a pretty small family. We met in college, and even back then she was off men."

She better be. All the men that weren't *him*. "You have no idea why?"

"You're going to have to ask her about it."

The waiting area was packed, and Theo realized, with a hard thud of his heart, that they could be here for hours. "Tell me more."

"She's the most positive person I know. A little absentminded. Would that bother you?" Her direct gaze was unsettling.

He scoffed. "No, why would it?" *Just as long as she doesn't forget me.*

"Some guys are weird about that stuff. Oh! And she has no sense of direction. Like, at all."

46

"Perfect. I'm a walking GPS. Go on."

"Funny, silly, gets lost in her thoughts a lot. Her mom was Mexican and her dad was European of some kind. But I think they both died when she was younger. Um, do you have any questions for me?"

"I did, but you said I should ask her."

She peered at him over her glasses. Brynn was a community college professor and at the moment he felt like he was back in school. "How come you aren't asking about her wigs?"

"Why would I?"

She checked him out a few seconds more and then smiled. "Good answer."

His Reina always looked perfect. His only hope was she wasn't sick. He couldn't... he couldn't handle something like that again. But she looked so healthy and vibrant. Her peaches and cream complexion glowed. He could spend hours dedicated to licking and kissing every inch of her.

Rein it in Romero—this is about Brynn.

"Over here." Reina waved to them from a side hallway. "I got you a room. But before you freak out and accuse me of cutting in line, they would have made you a priority, regardless. I moved the paperwork through faster than most."

Theo was grateful when they made it to her private room, and he could place Brynn in bed. Mission accomplished. Except, now what? He stood awkwardly and looked to Reina.

She was in her element. "I'm going to check and see who's working the emergency room today. I'll be right back," Reina said.

"I'll be in the waiting room." He tried not to wince.

"It's okay. You can wait in the car if you're more comfortable," she said as she rushed out.

Brynn grasped his hand as he turned to go. "Thank you, Theo. I appreciate your help."

"No problem."

"I'm gonna find a way to pay you back." She pulled up the blankets and settled back in bed.

"For taking you to the hospital?"

"No. Because you saved my Alexei." A suspicious sheen of liquid coated her eyes.

"What?" He rubbed his chest, feeling uncomfortable with the emotion that sat heavy in the room. "That was nothing."

"It wasn't, and I really appreciate it." She sniffled. "Ignore me. I have baby hormones, and Alexei's probably hijacking a plane to get back home."

"Probably." He huffed. "Your man is ridiculously dramatic, but he loves you with everything he has."

"I know. I'm so lucky." She patted his arm and let go of his hand. "Remember what I said. I already have an idea about what I'm going to do."

Theo scrubbed his hand down his face. "I'm afraid to ask."

"My friend is beautiful, inside and out. I'm hoping you don't mess it up if she gives you a chance."

He fisted his hands. "She's... everything."

"That's what I thought." She smiled and greeted the nurse, who came in with a thermometer and a blood pressure cuff.

Time to go. Gracias a dios.

"You'll know when the opportunity presents itself." Brynn waved him off. "Be ready."

Chapter 8

COOCH SMOOCH

"HOW LONG DO you think they'll keep me?" Brynn worried her lip.

"I don't know. The doctor will be in soon to go over it, but I think there may be a small chance they'll keep you overnight." Ren walked over to the white board hanging on the wall, checking to see which nurses had been assigned to Brynn.

"Why? Because of my blood pressure? It's never been that high before." She twisted the gold band on her finger. "I can't believe it. It's been a little higher than normal at my visits but nothing like what they said."

"Listen, this is a stressful situation. You took a fall. We practically flew here with the way Theo was driving… It's a lot." Ren wished she were exaggerating but that man was a maniac, even though he thought he'd been super-careful.

Brynn laughed softly, her face looking a little less strained.

"Most people's blood pressure goes up in a hospital."

"You too?"

"Me? Nah. This is my happy place, so I get relaxed. But I practically live here so… I mean, there are a lot of rough days, but I hold on to the fact that most people will come out of here feeling better."

"Are you insane? Happy place? Who thinks like that?" Ai Zhao, Ren's newest bestie, sauntered into the room like she owned it—and hated it, all at once.

Ren loved Ai. They'd recently bonded at the charm school's Christmas auction. After that fated meeting, Ren had been granted entrance into Ai's inner circle. Which wasn't as hard as she let on. Ai didn't hate people anywhere near as much as she claimed. *Maybe?*

"This place gives me anxiety."

"Ai, what are you doing here?" Brynn held open her arms and Ai rushed into them, hugging her for a long time.

"Dacey, sent me." She adjusted the messy bun atop her hair. She was decked out in ripped jeans and a paint strewn sweatshirt. She looked as lovely as ever. "Your sister gave me strict instructions to do whatever I had to, to save your life. Kidney, lung, heart. Baby D is crazy." Ai used the monikers given the Quads when they were in the womb. Babies A, B, C and D. "I don't understand what she says half the time."

Both of the other two women nodded in agreement. The youngest of the Calvo Quads was *cray-cray.*

"How long till I can bust you out?" Ai shuddered when she accidentally brushed up against the baby's heart monitor.

"I don't know. We're waiting for the doctor to come in and let us know what she thinks."

"By the way, you do realize there's a pouty serial killer hunkered down in the waiting room?"

"Who? Theo? I told him he could wait in the car. He likes hospitals about as much as you." Ren frowned. "And he doesn't look like a serial killer."

"Oh really? Then how did you know who I was talking about?"

"I... You might have a point." Ren giggled and put Brynn's chart behind the door.

"He looks like he's going to murder someone or hyperventilate.

50

That can't be good, right?" Ai gently adjusted Brynn's pillow and tucked her blanket under her arms. "I think he made an old lady cry. I swear." She sat next to Brynn and grabbed her hand.

Ren rolled her eyes. "He's not that bad."

"*Puhleeze*. I don't know what you see in him. He looks mean."

"He's not. He's actually pretty funny and super smart." Brynn adjusted her glasses and smiled at Ai. "But his past has been… challenging."

"Omigosh. He's so complicated. It only makes him sexier." Ren bypassed the monitors and maneuvered to the opposite side of the bed, grabbing Brynn's other hand.

"Yeah. Shouldn't you hate him, Brynn? Didn't he put your baby daddy, Alexei, in the hospital?"

"I should, but I don't. And he did." She smiled. "He hurt him to help him, which sounds abusive, but I swear it all makes sense. He and Alexei grew up together. They were like brothers, but something really tragic happened that split them apart. Theo blamed Alexei for the accident and hated him for years. They both started fighting for," Brynn looked around and whispered, "*la mafia*. Theo only did it so he could fight Alexei. It's a whole thing, but after they finally talked it out… well, first they beat the heck out of each other—then they talked it out and made things right."

"Did you seriously say *heck*? You're a grown woman." Ai rolled her eyes.

"Shh, stop interrupting her story." Ren leaned in, fascinated. She wanted to soak in every detail, every nuanced nugget of info that would help her understand how the grumpy Cuban operated.

He is devastatingly sexy.

"What happened next?" Ren prodded.

"Well, when Alexei and I got serious, he needed help getting out of *la mafia*. Because once you fight for *them*," she whispered again, "you're in for life. Or until they don't need you anymore."

"And the Cuban helped him leave?" Ai tightened her lopsided

bun.

"Yeah, he devised the plan to make sure Alexei was useless to them. But it entailed Alexei getting hurt. Alexei agreed, willing to do anything at that point. I hated the plan—he got so hurt, but it all worked out in the end."

"Wow." Ren had so many questions. What was the tragic accident? How had Theo hurt him? What was his sign? A thousand others bumped through her brain, but before she could ask, the doctor came in.

Ai and Ren stepped outside to let the doctor do her thing. She was a resident but very thorough.

"Are you going to talk to him?" Ai whispered.

"Who, Theo? No. I mean, I'm not going to *not* talk to him. He has to drive me back to the charm school to get my car." Ren cocked her head to the side. "Wait, what do you mean?"

Ai snickered. "You like him."

"What's not to like? He's gorgeous and frowny, and he knows how to outwit *la mafia*. Tell me that's not sexy."

"I guess. If you're into that sort of thing." Ai crossed her arms and leaned against the wall. "But please keep in mind that he got Alexei out, but *he's* still in. He fights for them. Do you want somebody in your life like that?"

"Why are you judging him so harshly? You don't know what led him to fight."

"Because I see how fascinated you are with him. I'm reserving judgment till I speak to him, but I'm trying to be the level-headed one. And I've never even seen you look twice at anybody but him. Your whole face is red right now. You look like a tomato."

"I do?"

Ai laughed. "A beautiful tomato." She hugged her. "You know I hate all people. Don't listen to me. But do. Because I'm worried about you."

"It doesn't matter. You know I'm not dating right now." Ren

pulled back, only slightly annoyed with her friend. Ai tried to pretend to be hardcore, but she was ooey-gooey on the inside, and she loved her friends. "It was nice of him to drive us here."

"I don't think 'nice' is the right word to describe him."

The doctor walked out, and they rushed back to Brynn.

"What did she say?" Ren asked, and then remembered Ai was there. She'd already obtained Brynn's permission to look over her medical records. "If you're not comfortable discussing this in front of Ai, she can wait outside."

"Ooh, I like your professional voice." Ai nodded. "And she's right. I can step out."

"No. It's okay. I'm here for observation, and the doctor wants me on bed rest until I see my own ob-gyn. But she thinks I may be off my feet for the rest of my pregnancy."

"Holy shit. That's tough." Ai rubbed her arm.

Ren knew how upset Baby B was because she didn't even giggle when Ai cursed. "Are you okay? Is there anything I can do?"

"Yes." Brynn pierced her with her hazel gaze. "I need you to teach the cunnilingus class for me."

Chapter 9

NINJALINGUS

THEO SUCKED IN a deep breath, fisting his hands but refusing to wuss out. He appreciated Reina's suggestion about waiting in the car, but his friend needed him to find out what was happening. Alexei was stuck, hours away, and he must be going fucking crazy.

So no, he wouldn't leave. No matter how much this place creeped him the hell out.

I might throw up.

His phone rang for the thousandth time. An older woman sitting across from him smiled gently, as if she understood his pain. "What?"

"Talk to me," Alexei demanded.

"Man, I wish I could. I don't know anything yet." Theo's leg wouldn't calm down, bouncing in total frustration. "It wouldn't be right for me to be in there when she's with the doc."

"I'm booking my flight home now," he growled.

"Look, *acere*. We talked about this. Give the professionals a chance to look her over." Theo looked at his watch. "It's only been a few hours since we got here."

"I know, it's…hospitals. Not a good head space for me."

"You know I understand that." Theo caught his breath, assailed by memories—seeing Rosie, the owner of his heart, and Alexei both severely burned had broken him. "I know," he whispered.

"Shit, I'm sorry, man. I'm putting you through hell."

"Nope, I got this. If I can stick it out in this waiting room, you can wait until Brynn gets back to you. No booking anything. Deal?" The sweet woman who was literally knitting in front of him, a bastion of calmness, nodded her head as if to offer her encouragement. It was nice. Most people were too afraid of him to engage.

Maybe I should work on that. Nah.

"Give me something. Go over to the room."

He heard the desperation in Alexei's voice and his memory of Rosie in the hospital, covered in burns, got him on his feet and heading toward Brynn's room. "Give me a minute."

As he rounded the corner, he saw Reina and Ai standing outside Brynn's room, arguing.

"I can't do it!" Reina threw her hands in the air.

"You have to," Ai responded, shrugging her shoulders as she quietly shut the door behind her.

Theo's spidey senses went off. Who was pressuring Reina?

"What's going on?" Alexei asked through the phone.

"Let me call you right back. Reina's standing outside the door."

"Call me the minute she tells you anything."

"I'm on it. *Chao pescao.*"

Theo walked up but the women took no notice.

"You do it." Reina grabbed Ai's arm.

"Hell no. You do *not* want me handling this situation. Teaching stupid men about shit they should already know how to do. Oh no, no, no. I'll go off." Ai looked annoyed, which was pretty much how she looked most days.

"You don't understand. I can't—"

Theo cleared his throat. "Uh, is everything okay?" *And who do I need to take out?* No one would force Reina to do anything she didn't want.

"Everything's fine." Ai narrowed her eyes as she walked up on him. "You still fighting for *la mafia?*"

Used to Ai's direct approach and appreciating it, he shrugged. "Undecided."

"What the hell does that mean?" Ai crossed her arms.

"Ai! That's none of our business."

"I'm asking because you won't." The ding of a high-pitched bell interrupted her. Ai pulled her phone out of her back pocket. "That's my house alarm. My stoner house guests, Jesus and Nacho, are probably burning the place down. Gotta go." She swept Reina up in her arms and kissed her on the cheek. "Good luck. With everything." She winked and walked away.

"Reina?" Theo approached cautiously, not sure if she was pissed or not. But he wanted to make it better. What was it about this woman? He hadn't been able to get her off his mind. They hadn't even spoken before yesterday, but... she was special. He knew it in his bones. Now all he had to do was convince her he was worthy.

The one flaw in my plan. "Everything okay?" He looked over his shoulder, but Ai was long gone.

"Ignore her." Reina reached toward him to touch his arm but froze and then dropped her hand. "Sorry. The good news is, the baby's fine."

The weight in his chest eased. Alexei would be able to breathe again. But wait... "That makes it seem like there's bad news, too."

"Yeah, there always is, isn't there?" A flash of sadness flitted across her large eyes until she looked down and waved it away. In seconds her sunny smile was back in place, but it looked strained.

"What's going on?" He crowded her in because he couldn't help himself.

"Nothing, nothing." She sighed. "Where were we?"

"Bad news."

"Right. The bad news isn't too bad. They're being cautious and want to observe her overnight."

"She has to stay here?" He shuddered and leaned against the white walls, needing the support. "Alexei's gonna freak."

"He won't when we explain that this is the best place for her. But…" she wrung her hands, "he might get upset about the next part."

"What is it?"

"It looks like they're going to put her on bed rest for the rest of the pregnancy."

"*Coño*. He's gonna come home. I know it. This trip is a big deal for him professionally." Theo scratched the side of his head in agitation. A bad habit he couldn't shake from childhood. "But wait, she has like *a hundred* sisters. They can help her, and he can stay up north till he finishes out the deal."

"No, they can't. They're all out of town, too. Well, except Athena, but she has a newborn. That's why I was going over to the charm school this weekend. I mean, besides the speed dating. Brynn thinks it was just to help go through some of Ms. Belle's paperwork, but it was also to keep an eye on her. Her sister, Dacey, called me because she was a little worried about Brynn pushing herself." Reina tapped her bag. "We can leave now. Visiting hours were over a long time ago."

They walked out to the car.

Theo's phone immediately rang. He looked down and groaned, reluctant to share the news. "That's him."

Ren held up her hand. "Don't answer that yet. Give me a minute to figure out how to handle him."

"Okay, but hurry because he'll probably call Brynn next." Theo stood next to her and blocked her from the cars whizzing through the parking lot, happy to be near her. She smelled amazing, like vanilla and spice.

"Okay." She took a deep breath. "I think I've got it. Call him back and give me the phone."

"*Se estará hecho un ají.* He'll be pissed. Get ready."

"I can handle it." She winked. "Don't worry."

I'm in love. His neglected cock swelled in his pants. He loved seeing confident Reina; it made him want to kiss the hell out of her. "What are you going to do?"

"Fix this." She swiped his phone and put it on speaker. "Hey, Alexei, it's Ren. Theo's here too."

"Why are you... *oh fuck.* It's bad. Tell me, Ren. Is it bad?"

"No, no. It's all really good. Please don't stress. I'll tell you everything the doctor said, I promise. Do you have a pen and paper, or can you take notes on your phone while I talk?'

"Why would I—"

"Because it's hard to remember the important stuff when it's a high-stress situation. I want you to be able to look back at your notes if you have any questions, or you're worried about something."

"Tell me." He paused. "I'm booking a flight now. I can't believe I waited. I should have—"

"Alexei. Listen to me. Brynn is fine. The baby is fine. You made the perfect choice. If Brynn had been worried about you coming back early, it would've made the situation ten times worse. She would've stressed out that she was costing you this opportunity. You've both worked so hard to get your lamps the attention they deserve."

Reina was absolutely amazing. She talked Alexei off the ledge, twisted him around her finger, and got him to agree to everything she suggested—in the sweetest way possible. It was unbelievable. Theo wouldn't have believed it if he hadn't witnessed it. He was half in a daze himself. She went through point by point, almost losing Alexei when she mentioned bed rest.

"All of her sisters are out of town! She'll push herself to make the class a success."

"No worries, because I'm going to be staying with her at the school. She…" Her steady voice faltered for the first time in the conversation. She glanced over at Theo and tried to walk away.

Theo followed.

Reina tensed but continued, "She wants me to teach the next class for her, so I'm going to stick around until then. Everybody else will be home after that."

"You would do that for her?"

"Of course. I love her. I love you both. I'd do anything to help you guys. And if I have to teach the class," she gripped his phone so hard, her fair hand went red, "then that's what I'll do."

Oh hell, yeah. This was it. Theo's in. If she was teaching the class on… what the hell was the next class about? Damn, she never told him. All he knew was the classes were notoriously down and dirty with tons of research, and if that was the case, Reina would need help. His help.

Thank you, Brynn.

Mission accepted. Even if she hadn't extended an invitation. Yet.

Chapter 10

VAGITARIAN

EARLY MONDAY MORNING

THE CAR RIDE back to the charm school had been quiet. Ren had gone radio silent. The girl who never shut up, couldn't stop thinking about teaching a cunnilingus class. For years, most of her nights were spent alone unless she had to work. Now, everything had changed—speed dating and VJ classes, all within a few days of her normally boring life.

"We're here," Theo's gruff voice filled the van. His hands gripped the steering wheel and he still looked a little pale.

Maybe I shouldn't have been thinking about myself. He was obviously going through something too. "Hey. Are you okay?"

"I need a minute." He closed his eyes and rested his head against the back of the seat. "Hospitals give me the spins."

"I'm sorry." She wanted to take his hand in hers, but she had no right to do that. He hadn't asked for her comfort. So much had happened since speed dating. All of it a painful reminder of the unfinished business that had controlled her life for years. *Time for a little happy.* "How about some trail mix?"

"What?" He blinked, finally opening his eyes.

"Food is love, right?" She laughed and rummaged around in her purse, hoping to distract him with her signature nonsense. "My absolute favorite is the Monster Mix. I like everything except the chocolate and butterscotch chips."

"Why don't you get the kind that doesn't have the chips?"

She sighed. "I've tried, Theo Romero, but it just isn't the same. I like the perfect combination of M&Ms, peanuts, and the most crucial and underappreciated ingredient of them all…raisins. Which on its own is unappealing but combined with the other two is…chef's kiss. Perfection." She brought her fingers to her lips and made the *mwah* kissy sound. "This batch may be chip heavy," she giggled and poured some in his hand, "because I eat the good stuff and throw the rest back in."

"Chocolate and butterscotch are my favorite." He picked out the chips and popped them in his mouth. Then he raised his hand, leaving her the rest. "For you."

Her eyes went wide and for the briefest second, she felt the most intense longing of her life. She wished she could *keep* him, not for a few hours or a day… but forever. And even as she tried to talk herself out of it, the feeling lingered. "I have one more thing in my bag of tricks that may work even better than trail mix."

"What?" He looked adorably dubious.

She pulled out her favorite stone. "This is amethyst. It's protective and is responsible for healing. It's really good at purging negative thoughts. I think it might help you."

"What do I do with it?"

"You hold it."

"That's it?" He studied the stone and shrugged. "Okay, thanks."

"You're welcome."

"You ready to tell me the truth? About running away from me last night?"

Damn. This man was like a dog with a bone. She contemplated asking about why he looked so miserable, but she couldn't do that to him—too personal, and obviously too painful. She chose the lesser of two evils because she was curious. And she didn't want to answer his question. "Why'd you stop all the guys from talking to me?"

"That's how you're going to play it?" His smart hazel eyes zeroed in on her. "I've got your number, Reina. Deflect, deflect, deflect."

Damn, maybe his high IQ went beyond just numbers. *If so, I'm in trouble.* "I was curious."

"So am I. How about we share info?" Theo brushed the crumbs from his hands.

"You first."

"Only if you hold my hand," he demanded in the most adorable way.

She lifted her eyebrow at him, but his frown hadn't budged. *Yes, please.* Dying to touch any part of him, she sighed dramatically to cover her eagerness. She gripped his hand tight with both of hers.

"Yes, I told Blue to keep the guys away."

"Why?"

"I told you. I wanted to talk to you. One-on-one. I tried to talk to you for *six* months. I wanted a chance for you to get to know me. But it's obvious you were pissed because you took off so fast."

She was floored… and overwhelmed that he'd made such an effort. She figured it was only fair to confess some of her truth. "I wasn't upset that you'd warned the guys off. The plan was to chat for the two minutes and that's it. I thought it was kind of sweet once I realized it wasn't me that made them avoid me like the plague. High-handed but sweet."

"You weren't mad?" His dark brows climbed his forehead. "Then why'd you bolt?" A small grin grew until it looked shark-like. "You were jealous of Viviana?"

"How *dare* you?" She smiled. "How could I be jealous of that gorgeous model you came to the speed dating with?" She couldn't meet his eyes.

"Model? *Her*? She's like the most annoying little sister you could ever have." He traced her cheek. "I can't believe you were jealous. She drives me insane."

"I believe you." Ren smiled, completely believing him but realizing she hadn't told him the whole story. "But there's a little bit more to it."

"What do you mean?"

She let out a breath. "She was more of a reminder of why I've been avoiding you."

"It's not because I'm scary looking?" There was a question in his eyes.

Little did he know that was what she liked about him. She loved his strong features and his quick wit, even the surly temper that usually wasn't directed at her. "You're not scary. You're sexy." Damn it. Why had she said that again?

"Reina, you're confusing the hell out of me. How am I supposed to resist you when you say things like that—and then end the best date I ever had?"

He's killing me. Who knew he'd be so sweet? The same man who looked like he intended to remove the heads of any guy who dared to talk to her during speed dating. A shiver went down her spine.

He's so hot. Devastatingly so.

"That's a fair question, so I'm going to be honest with you. I like you."

"You do?"

"I do." Ren nodded. "And if circumstances were different, I'd want to get to know you."

"*Coño.* I don't want to hear the rest." His head went back to rest against the seat.

"I'm sorry." She absently rubbed her palm over the top of his, loving the feel of his rough hands. "My life is ridiculously complicated, and I have a lot going on. Including teaching this class."

His body went rigid. "What's the next class about?" He was trying for nonchalant but she understood what was happening immediately.

"Oh no," she shook her head, "I'm not telling you."

"I can find out in two seconds if I want to. Come on. Tell me. Maybe I can help you out."

Her whole face flushed as she imagined the sexiest man she'd ever met, going down on her for five whole days. She was equally mortified and excited. He... he...

"Reina?"

A cascade of visuals punched through her mind. Her on the bed, spread eagle. Him completing impossible feats of strength by lifting her on his shoulders and going to town.

"*Reina?*"

"What?" She blinked and zeroed back in on him.

"Let me help." His voice dropped to a growl. "I know you're thinking about it right now. Tell me. Tell me what I can help you with, and I'm all yours."

"I can't. I'm sorry." She grabbed her bag and opened the passenger side door. "Thanks for the ride."

He stared at her, obviously frustrated with her answer. "At least let me walk you in and make sure it's safe."

"It's a charm school. I think it'll be okay." But she studied him and before she shut the door, said, "But if it makes you feel better, come on in."

"Are you staying here tonight?" He walked her to the back door.

"No. I have to go home and get all of my stuff for the week."

"It's late." The fierce frown was back. "I don't like the idea of you driving at this time of night."

Ren laughed. *Aww.* Silly boy. "I'm a grown woman who drives around all the time at night. But, that's sweet and kind of crazy."

"Yeah, I've been told."

"You're a worrier, huh?"

"Only about the important people. The rest of the world can go fuck themselves."

Ren burst out laughing, understanding that the man standing in front of her was slightly insane. Most people would be put off by his semi-controlling ways and foul mouth. But she loved it. She sensed he was being his authentic self. Maybe deep down inside, she secretly wished she were one of those special people. Right now, he was being polite—yet broadcasting his need with every glance.

Bliss.

"What do you have to pick up?" He followed her back inside to Ms. Belle's office.

"The instruction manual." The small office wasn't much more than a love seat and big table. Warm and inviting. A huge travel trunk sat in the corner. "Brynn has been going old-school and hand writing suggestions from Ms. Belle's original information. Along with some diagrams. I don't know. It's all too much." Ren snapped her mouth shut. She'd revealed way too much.

When she glanced over at him, he was leaning into the room, his hands braced on the sides of the doorframe. The man oozed sex appeal. God, it made everything south of her waist melt.

But his eyes, they were alive with something intangible. He kept his gaze fixed on her as she opened the lid of the trunk. "You ready to tell me what it's about?"

Her body tensed, but she accepted she wouldn't be able to change the subject, so she mumbled, "Cunnilingus."

"I'm sorry, what?" He cocked his head to the side.

She grabbed the notebook and folder marked Cunny Class, and slammed the lid shut. "Cunn-i-lin-gus!" She stood at the door, fully prepared to walk indignantly from the room, but he wouldn't budge.

"Why are you yelling the word cunnilingus at me?" His frown dropped and the playful smile emerged.

"Because you heard me the first time."

"I did. But I thought it must be my imagination. That's the best word I've ever heard you say. Plus, I like to see you blush."

Ren's cheeks flushed brighter. Of course, he must love going downtown. He had a tongue piercing. Dear Lord, what that must feel like. She roused herself and gestured toward his hulking mass blocking the door. "I'm ready to go. Thanks."

"I want to help."

"No."

"Why not?"

"I don't even know you, and you want to go down on me?"

"*Coño*, that would be a fucking dream." A muscle in his cheek ticked. "Hell yes, I do."

"Who says stuff like that?"

"Men. To beautiful women they're attracted to." He stepped toward her, his chest swelling. "I would worship you, Reina. Go down for hours and never touch myself once. I'd make you come so many times you'd lose count."

Her eyes went wide and the room spun for a moment. The fire in his eyes consumed her, made her believe every word. But... but... he didn't understand that wasn't something she had any experience in. The one time had been so awkward she'd never wanted to try it again.

"Thank you, but no."

"*Thank you?* Why are you talking to me like I'm one of your clients at the hospital? Reina." His deep voice roughened. "Let me help you with this."

"I can't. I'm sorry." This time she rushed past him and he let her. What could she say? That her clit didn't respond well to anything but her vibrator? Or should she tell him the real reason she was running? Because if there had ever been someone on the planet who tempted her, it was Theo Romero.

Ren made it out to the back door and impatiently waited for

him to follow so she could lock up.

"That's it? Just thank you and *no*?" His voice rose with each word.

She spun around, and the folder flew out of her hand. Rudimentary drawings of women's vaginas, with pen marks all over them, fluttered around her. She bent down to retrieve the drawings. "I'm sorry. I'm not trying to... I can't get involved right now. I have someone in my life—"

"You're fucking somebody?" Theo paused in the middle of helping her, his scowl reappearing but doing nothing to hide his hurt.

"No! No, I'm not sleeping with anybody, but I do have some serious commitments and responsibilities." She dropped the folder and looked at Theo. She couldn't help herself. Her need to please usually kicked in, that incessant need to say anything to make people feel better. This was different. She needed to be honest with him. He deserved the truth. "I promise you, if I could choose anyone to help me with this class, it would be you."

He grabbed her hands and tugged her closer. "Then do it."

"I can't." Her voice caught.

His intense gaze bore deep, his frown becoming more and more pronounced. "Let me see if I have this straight. If you could pick someone, it would be me?"

"Yes."

"No one else is going to help you with the class?"

She shook her head, owing him no explanations but wanting to get the hurt look off his face.

"Not even the 'someone' you have in your life? They're not going to help you with research?"

She smiled and appreciated his sneaky mind. He was still trying to figure this all out and she loved it. Loved everything about this moment. The feel of him, the warmth of his huge palms engulfing her own. "Nope. It'll be me and the notebook and charts. Whatever the heck they were." She made a face and he actually smiled.

But then the intense look was back. He studied every inch of her face and eventually nodded. "I understand."

It made her sad because that meant she wouldn't be able to hold his hands anymore. And she liked doing that. Too much.

"I have one more request." He cupped her face, his thumb brushing her cheek. "Kiss me goodbye."

"But…"

"If this is the last time we see each other, I want a kiss."

"The last time we see each other?" Like a knife to the heart, his words cut deep.

"Let me put it this way. I'm not coming back here. That means if you want me, you're going to have to come and get me." For some reason, his frown disappeared, and the playful grin was back.

Super suspicious.

Ren didn't hesitate and threw her arms around his neck, slamming her mouth against his. She took advantage of his surprised gasp and slipped her tongue between his pillow lips. Never had she kissed someone like this and never had it been this good.

His strong arms banded around her back, pulling her off her feet as they smashed their lips together, grinding and brushing and *devouring* each other. His piercing rolled against her tongue, heightening her awareness of him. It wasn't a shared moment; it was a battle and she loved it. Because Ren meant it when she said she'd choose him every time. Circumstances prohibited it, and it pissed her off.

Pulling back with a pop, she licked her bottom lip to savor his taste.

"*Jesus Christ.* You're killing me." He ran his hand through his hair.

Ren shoved everything she could see in her bag and ignored his softly spoken words. They locked up and trudged back to her car. After getting inside, she rolled down her window.

"Fuck, Reina. We'd be so good together. That kiss…" he murmured as he bent over and rested his elbow on her driver's side door. "I look forward to number two."

"You know that was a goodbye kiss."

"Maybe. Or maybe we'll see each other sooner than you think." He winked. The playful smile back.

"What? Why?"

"Ball's in your court. See you soon."

Chapter 11

YODEL IN THE VALLEY

TUESDAY

"YOU ALL COMFY?" Ren carefully patted down the paper pieced quilt, tucking in her exasperated friend. The small bedroom, located at the back of the house, was perfectly located. Not far from the exit and no stairs. Plus, The Ladies, a group of octogenarians who ran the school, would be able to visit as much as they liked.

"I'm perfect. Stop fussing. You're worse than Alexei," Brynn huffed, and pointed toward the small desk. "Can you hand me my laptop?"

"Were you able to get someone to cover your classes?" Brynn was a community college professor at East Los Angeles College.

"Yes, two were online, so I'll keep those. I have subs for the other three. I may be stuck in bed, but it looks like I'll still be working part time." Her sunny smile showed how much she loved her job. "Don't you have to work today?"

"Nope. I have Sundays and Mondays off. You're stuck with me."

"Ren. This is ridiculous. What are you going to do, watch me sleep? I'll be perfectly fine. The Ladies will keep me company during the day and then I'll go to bed."

"Watching you sleep? How is that possible if we're having a slumber party? I'll bring my sleeping bag, and we can camp out." She laughed, and Brynn giggled with her. "Seriously, it's no big deal. You'll probably be sexting with your baby daddy anyway. I'll be here to check in on you."

"And researching for the class. Right?"

Crickets.

"Right? You said you'd teach the class, *right?*"

"Yes! I said I'd do it," Ren grumbled and grabbed her bag. She pulled out the file with the weird sketches. "What's with these drawings?

"Oh, I got those from a professor who teaches Human Sexuality at my school. Those are basic drawings of the female anatomy. Here, hand me one." She pointed at the two curved lines on either side. "These are the thighs, this dot is where the clitoris is and then the small X under it represents the vaginal canal, and then this dot is the back door action."

The small lines and circles were so rudimentary it didn't look weird or personal. It was like stick figures of girly parts.

"Got it." She squinted at the paper. "What's with the scribbles all over them?"

"That's the best part." Brynn held one up. "They asked twenty-five guys and then twenty-five women to show how to give proper VJs. Look at what some of the guys put. This guy has every orifice circled and all he wrote was lick, lick, lick over and over again."

"Dear Lord, this guy acts like he's supposed to tear the thing off. Ouch!" They screamed laughing.

"Then here are twenty-five bisexual or lesbian women who talk about how they give and receive it."

Worlds apart.

"You ready to go over the rest? Where's the notebook? I literally have a whole lesson plan for you. I want you to read through it because you're going to get a lot of questions. And of course, firsthand knowledge is even better." Brynn winked.

Heat blazed across Ren's neck and cheeks. She sighed, knowing exactly where this conversation was headed and wishing with all her might she was wrong. "You know I don't have someone in my life right now."

"I do know that, but I don't know why."

Panic seized her. All roads lead back to her devastatingly sexy Cuban. *No, not mine. Not mine.* "Brynn."

"Come on. Talk to me. Is it that you aren't interested in Theo? If so, I get it. Just because he's obsessed with you doesn't mean you're into him."

Ren stopped searching for the cunny book and stared at her friend in disbelief. "You think he's obsessed with me?" She couldn't keep the squeal out of her voice. He'd showed her a million different ways, but she still couldn't believe a sex-god like Theo was really into her.

"A ha! See. You like him. Why don't you give him a chance? Is it the fighting stuff? The tatts, the piercings, the muscles...what?" Brynn's cheesy grin gave her away, clearly not as neutral as she'd like to seem. "I've known you awhile now, and even though we only reconnected a few months ago, I've never seen you react the way you do around Theo."

"I know. You're right. I haven't."

"You said you hadn't dated since high school."

She nodded, a familiar tightness seizing her chest and arms. Brynn was setting up for the hard questions, and she wasn't sure if she was ready to go there.

"Why not?"

Well shit, she hadn't expected her to be so direct.

"I think you know a little bit about my boyfriend from high school and how he was in a really bad accident." Ren's mind swam when she dipped back into that time period, the worst of her life. There was no way she could manage contemplating Theo, teaching this class, living at the charm school, and reliving these memories, but she was ready to share some of it with Brynn. Maybe she could give Ren some perspective. Because unintentionally or not, Theo had pushed her to a breaking point with that kiss, and something had to change.

"I remember you telling me about it once. But not much detail."

"This is what I'll say because it's still hard to talk about." She grabbed one of Ms. Belle's inspirational pillows which read: Life's a beach. Enjoy the waves. "He got into a horrible motorcycle accident."

"I'm so sorry."

"Everything about that night changed my life." Images of the last minutes before he'd zoomed off on his motorcycle. She'd devastated him. Broken up with him. The next time she'd seen him, Nicholas had been in a hospital bed, hooked up to a ventilator. "But what I don't think you know is… he survived."

"He did?"

"Yes. He's been in a coma for years." It all felt like it was happening yesterday, and worst of all, she could never explain the guilt she associated with that night. She felt bad even thinking about it, let alone talking about it. But she could share some of it so Brynn understood. "His mom is so devoted to him. He doesn't have much family, like me. So she's his everything. She's an amazing woman and has never lost hope that he'll come out of this."

"Is that what you think?"

"I've decided," she took a deep breath, "that I have to love Nicholas for who he is now, and cherish that he's with us in some way. But no, I don't think he'll ever return to who he was. But because his mom is so devoted, I can't… I would never want to hurt her." She rubbed her forehead. "Oh God, I'm messing this all up."

"Ren, are you saying that you aren't dating anyone because of his mom?"

"No... I mean, listen, first of all, I haven't been ready. It's been my choice. None of this is on her, but I would never want to add to her pain."

Brynn sat for a moment, simply gazing at her and nodding. "I hear you. I totally understand your feelings and your choices."

Ren chewed on her thumbnail as Brynn's words soaked in. Some of her tension dissipated. Brynn understood, and she knew it was the right thing to do, which meant—*Oh God, my decision to avoid Theo was the right one.*

"But... I also understand that deep down, you know your actions aren't healthy long-term."

The breath Ren had been holding whooshed out of her mouth.

"I see how devoted you are to the patients in the hospital. What would you tell one of them if they shared a similar story? Would you advise them to shut themselves off to love and companionship? Is that what your ex would have wanted?"

Ren dropped her head in her hands. "No. Of course not."

"I think you've sidelined yourself because of what happened. Survivor's guilt, along with a ton of other worries and responsibilities, are interwoven into these kinds of events. You survived. You lived. And that's a beautiful thing. Don't give up your chance at happiness."

Silent tears tracked down Ren's face. Leave it to Brynn to sum up her life so precisely and beautifully.

"I'm so sorry you've carried this burden." Matching tears wet Brynn's eyes. "You deserve to be happy. I want that for you. It doesn't mean it has to be with Theo, but think about how you feel around him."

"I'm like a horny puppy dog, following him around and kissing him kind of violently."

"You did? Wait, why violently?" Brynn blinked and burst into laughter.

The two of them giggled, and Ren fell on her side, not knowing if she was sobbing or laughing anymore. Slowly, she sat up and wiped the tears from her face.

"I think because he frustrates me, and *I* frustrate me… and he has a tongue ring, and it felt *so good*. He was bossing me around, which I should hate, but I secretly love. He also had Blue keep all the guys from talking to me at speed dating." She sighed.

"You *like* that? It's kind of high-handed." Brynn sighed. "But I have to admit Alexei can be the same. What's up with these boys?"

"I know, right? He's a total control freak. But I love it, within reason. Can you… can you imagine what that would mean about him in bed?" She waved her hands in front of her face to cool herself off. "I don't have a lot of experience, so for me, that's hot."

"Ren, it seems like if you were ever ready, it's now. Don't let the past control you. Take this opportunity. I don't know if you've realized this but all four of us, my sisters and I, have found our true loves because of this charm school and these classes." Brynn swiped a finger under her glasses to wipe off the tears. "I like to think Ms. Belle's pulling some strings for us up there. But these chances, and the right people, don't come around that often."

"Teach the class with Theo and let him…" Ren winced. "That sort of leads me to the second reason I can't teach this class."

"Why?"

"I don't have a lot of great experience with a guy going downtown." Ren pointed at her girly parts, and they both howled with laughter.

"That's okay. I don't think he'd mind showing you the ropes. And if he sucks at it, that's what we have the notebook for. Go get it, and we'll look over it together."

"How do I even bring up something like that? To him?"

"When I was talking Alexei into helping me with the class, we played Truth or Dare Poker. That kind of turned into a make-out session, but it let us get to know each other and set parameters on what we were comfortable with."

"Did you say *you* had to talk Alexei into helping you?" Ren grabbed her bag and searched inside.

"Oh yeah, it was the fight of my life. Caelen made me promise to fight porn star dirty." Brynn blushed. "He eventually met me halfway, but it was a long road getting there. It looks like Theo has put in the time, over six months, right? The only question is, are you ready to meet him halfway? If not, then put him out of his misery."

"But it's too late. Last night we shared a goodbye kiss. Shoot."

PING.

"What's the matter?"

"I can't find the manual. The Cunny Book." She looked around.

"When was the last time you saw it?"

"Last night when I was talking to…" Theo's playful grin popped into her mind.

Oh no.

"I'm sure it's around here somewhere."

PING.

Ren looked down at the cell but didn't pick it up.

"What's the matter?"

"I don't have a good feeling about this." She eventually swiped the phone because she couldn't stand it another minute. Sure enough, there were two new text messages. When she opened it, the first was a photo of the notebook. The second, a four word message:

Come and get it.

Chapter 12

GIVE FACE

"*Toma!* The bigger they are, the harder they fall." Theo slammed his hand into his opponents' glass jaw, watching him go down after a few minutes in the ring. The guy sort of spun and then landed with a loud *thunk*. Theo clenched his teeth and looked around the gym. "Who's next?"

The small group of gym heads, the ones who'd been leaning over the ropes to get a better idea of his techniques, all took a few steps back.

"Come on, chumps. I'm just getting started."

"Hell no, man. You fight dirty."

"Who said that?" Theo snarled, and eyed the group. No one raised a hand. "What?" *Say it to my face.*

Blue walked over and high-fived a few of the guys. "All right, everybody. Almost closing time. Hit the showers. I'll see you tomorrow." Waiting a few minutes until the guys cleared out, he rounded on Theo. "Those are paying customers, asshole. Stop scaring them because you've got your panties in a bunch."

"My panties are fine, *pendejo*." Theo toed the guy on the floor who groaned, confirming he was still alive. "You told me to train them. How else will they learn if they don't go head-to-head in a real fight?"

Blue threw a towel at Theo. "Take five with me in my office. Hey, Viviana!" Blue called to the bored teen. "Make sure everything's locked up while I have a chat with *El Cubano* over here."

"Whatever." She waved him off and went back to her phone.

Blue headed toward the offices of the state-of-the-art gym. Theo had to admit, the place was sweet—an MMA fighter's dream. All the best equipment, training rooms, and some of the best professional-level instructors to run the classes.

Too bad some of the members are chumps and can't fight worth a damn.

Oh well, not *mi maletín.* It reminded him why he usually wouldn't step foot in a place like this. Except, Tommy, the owner and Blue's brother, was his friend, and he'd do just about anything for that crazy ginger.

Except change who I am. Which is what Blue seemed to expect him to do while coaching these lightweights. Where would he be if he'd been coddled? If his trainers had gone easy on him? Not that he'd had many. The first time he'd fought and won was because of sheer luck. He'd battled his way through the streets as a kid and literally learned MMA techniques from observing and then paying the price. The first time he'd been dumb enough to step in a ring had been brutal.

His muscles had screamed in pain, so much so he'd barely been able to walk the next day—*but he'd won.* That match and every single match since. He never lost, not because he was the best but because he'd studied the art of the MMA fighting. And he'd wanted it the most.

"What the hell, man? We've talked about this." Blue sprawled out behind his desk and flipped his cap backward. "I thought we agreed *not* to kill the customers."

"Tommy asked me to come and train the guys, and now you're giving me shit for it." Theo crossed his arms and spread his legs wide, his favorite "don't fuck with me," stance.

"Yeah, because you're a damn good fighter." Blue's usual smirk was missing. "My brother and I thought you might want to take your fighting in a different direction. Actually train people and stop messing with those stupid underground fights. They're gonna catch up with you."

"I'm good. Don't worry about me."

"But I do. I know you have a hell of a lot more going on than fighting in those death matches. You're the smartest guy I know. Why still fight for *them?* I thought the whole reason you originally did it was to get even with Alexei. You guys are good now. Why keep doing it?"

"I have my reasons." Like the fact that if he didn't have the fights to distract him, to *challenge* him, he would obsess. He needed a constant focus to keep from wallowing in the past, the pain still so intense his brain wouldn't shut off, it would only relive the worst moments of his life. He kept training and fighting, every day, until his brain and body collapsed. "No worries. I'm good."

"If you say so." Blue looked at him with knowing eyes. "I tried to talk to you about this before. Does this have anything to do with—"

"No!"

"Uh-huh." He grinned and sat up. "Which tells me it has everything to do with Ren. Come on, talk to me, man. It can't hurt, right?"

"Everything hurts eventually."

"Talk. Now. I got nowhere to be." Blue looked down at his watch. "Shit. I lied. I'm late for a date, but I want to hear from you first."

Theo sighed, understanding he may need a little help. "Fine. It's Ren."

"You saw her at the hospital with Brynn, right?" Blue had been Theo's second call, after Alexei. "Did you frown the whole time? Scare her off? Damn it. What did I tell you about that?"

"She's not afraid of me." Theo sighed and threw himself into the chair across from Blue's desk. "She's going to teach the next class."

"*What?*" Blue sat up. "This is your in. Offer to help her with it. Wait, what's the topic?" He rubbed his hands together in glee. "I can't wait."

"The word's too big for your pea brain to understand."

Blue barked out a laugh and shook his head. "Always the smart-ass. Come on, dumb it down for me."

"It's fucking ambrosia, heaven on earth… going down on your woman until she screams." Theo tensed as image after image of him feasting between his Reina's thighs assailed him.

"*My God.* Never a more perfect activity on the face of the planet." Blue also spaced out, obviously getting up close and personal with his imagination. Shaking it off, he looked over and smirked. "This is it. Help her teach the class. That's how Alexei got his girl, remember?"

"Which class was that?"

"Sex Toys, I think. It was before I got back to town, so I missed that one. Alexei said it was amazing." Blue slapped the desk. "It's fate. Stop acting like you usually do, and try and woo her."

"Woo her, huh?" He stretched his tight shoulders. "Shows what you know. I already tried and failed miserably."

"What'd you do? Did you pull out all the stops: flowers, chocolates… romantic poems?" Blue actually looked hopeful, as if there were any chance in hell Theo would do those things.

"No."

"Well, what'd you do?"

"I stole her instructional manual." Theo quickly scratched his head. "And then I sent her a text. No, I sent two." He held up two fingers.

"You're an idiot. That's your plan?" Blue opened the drawer and took out his keys and wallet. "Well? Did it work?"

"Does it look like it worked? I haven't heard from her. So, no."
He'd had a plan. It gave her a chance to chase him for once. But as
the minutes ticked by, he realized he'd been wrong. Again.

"Pathetic. Take my word for it. Woo. Her. Stealing or whatever
the hell you did isn't gonna work." Blue strode over to the door.
"After you hit the showers, don't forget to lock up. You got your
key?"

"In my locker. I'll take care of it. See you tomorrow."

Chapter 13

BOX LUNCH

REN LOOKED AROUND the working-class neighborhood, focusing in on a nondescript building with a blaring new sign that read, Tommy's Place. She'd heard about the grand opening of the gym a few months back but hadn't been able to attend. A tiny part of that may have been because of work, but a bigger part was because hanging by herself had become her new jam.

Over the years, she'd attended fewer and fewer parties, rejected more offers to go out and have fun. Besides the charm school classes and work, she hadn't been anywhere besides the hospital and home.

Can't avoid this forever. She didn't know where to begin to process her emotions toward the sneaky Cuban. He'd stolen her instructional manual and all he said was, *Come and get it?* Her head warred with her heart and her girly parts. He'd stolen her manual, but she wanted to see him so much her chest felt tight with need. *This is bad.* Really, really bad.

She was standing outside a gym in a sketchy neighborhood at close to midnight.

The chat with Brynn had changed everything. But now, her hastily constructed plan to have a light fling, and let him help her teach the class, sounded ridiculous. Did she want to get down and dirty in every conceivable position? With Theo Romero? *Pretty much.* Did she want him to rock her world by eating her out like a champ? *Maybe.*

She had no doubt about Theo's level of talent… it was her. Things hadn't worked out very well for her in the past. Embarrassment and worry would probably ruin the whole thing.

But the intensity of the way he looked at her—*kissed* her—made her knees weak. Plus, that tongue ring. God help her, she wanted to know what that felt like…*everywhere.* The chemistry was earth-shattering, but that didn't mean the rest of their lives would match up. Relationships couldn't last based on concentrated attraction alone. Could they?

Either way, it was time to get to know Theo a little better without putting any pressure on the relationship. Or whatever it was. A getting to know you type thing.

She raised her hand to knock when the door flung open, and a shocked teenager glared at her.

"Be careful! I almost dropped my phone," Viviana screeched and halted in front of Ren. She narrowed her eyes at Ren. "I know you."

"Yeah, we met at speed dating. Remember?"

"Right. You're the one who was, like, practically making out with Theo in front of everybody."

"I wasn't—"

"Whatever. I'm over it. I have a new boyfriend. Sort of." The tough exterior dropped for a millisecond, and Ren noticed vulnerability behind her oversized lashes. "Theo's in the back. Tell him to lock up, and don't forget. Blue will be so pissed at me if it's not done." She sped past, not waiting for an answer.

"Sure. Okay, bye!" Ren called and spun back around toward the glass entrance. In theory, this should be easy. Open the door, walk through the gym, find Theo, tell him off by peppering his face with kisses, and then retrieve the manual. But now none of that seemed so simple.

Ren peeked through the gym, impressed with how big and clean it was. She'd expected to be overpowered by the smell of dirty socks and jock straps, but the place was airy and much newer than she expected.

Making her way through, she passed individual training rooms along with a huge boxing ring that dominated the back half of the place. She ran her finger along the ropes, because she was curious and *not* trying to delay her meeting with Theo. The place looked deserted.

In a dark corridor, she stumbled through the darkened room, realizing she was surrounded by metal. Which meant, oh dear Lord…showers, steam. She'd landed in the locker room. Before she could backtrack, she came face to face with a Cuban god, sitting on a bench, with only a towel wrapped around his hips.

She would have salivated over his wide chest and intricate tattoos, except he wasn't stomping around and frowning, like usual. Instead, he sat with his head in his hands, looking completely…

Lost.

Without a second thought, Ren walked over, tempted to move his hands and sit in his lap. But she didn't have those privileges.

Not yet.

Recognizing pain was a big part of her job. Helping people get through the worst of it had become her specialty. She'd never thought of him as a client, but she could help him now if he was hurting.

"Theo?"

"Reina?" He blinked his hazel eyes and straightened.

"Yes, it's me." She cleared her throat. "Are you okay?"

"No." He scowled, looking as if he were upset with her. "I missed you."

"You missed me?" Ren melted into a pile of goo. The cavity

where her heart beat was now filled with a puddle of happiness.

"Yes! Why the hell do you think I stole your book?"

"But you knew I'd come." She stepped closer, her heart pounding an erratic beat. "Here I am."

He rested his arms on his legs and studied her face for a long time. "It's in my locker."

She hesitated, tempted to rush him, but realizing he'd cut her off, dismissed her, even though he'd said he missed her.

Am I too late?

"Uh, thanks." Although that was a stupid thing to say because he'd stolen the manual from *her*. She walked over and took a minute to study his messy locker. She especially liked that his clothes smelled like him, musky and full of his cologne, which reminded her of their intense kiss.

"What are you doing?"

Taking one last whiff. "Sorry, I was looking at your photos." There were four pics in a row of Theo and a dark-haired girl making funny poses in an old-fashioned photo booth.

Theo looked so young and happy.

Ren turned, shivering, because they were inches apart. She tried to look away, not really, but how could she resist? She'd never seen such wide shoulders and solid muscles. All painted in the most beautiful black ink.

He growled, "How am I supposed to *not* kiss you when you look at me like that?"

"I'm sorry. I can't help it." Her eyes ran the length of him. "I love your tattoos. And muscles." She sighed.

"Stop apologizing." He grabbed her thighs. With one tug, she stood in front of him, her hands on his shoulders. "You want to touch me? Do it. And tell me why you're really here."

"You're so bossy." But she obeyed, sighing as she ran her palms over his wide shoulders, kneading the thick muscles.

He dropped his head back, his whole body relaxing. It turned into a massage, and she took advantage of every second she had. Learning him with her hands, feeling him relax in front of her, she could do it for hours.

"*More.*"

"Why are you letting me do this to you?"

"Because I've wanted you to touch me for a long time." His burning hazel eyes zeroed in on her, and she bit her lip. "But I also want you to get to know me. To touch me like this wherever you want *if...*"

There's always a catch.

"You tell me you'll give us a chance. I can only take so much. I've been speeding headfirst into a wall with you for six months. And now that I've actually talked to you, felt your soft lips and amazing tongue, I want everything. No more starts and stops."

Her hands stilled. Sneaky fighter. Getting her addicted to his skin, *his smell*, and it was working. She wanted more, too. "That's fair, and it's why I'm here. I want to get to know you. And you, me. I should probably explain a few things. But..." She ran her eyes over the cut of his six-pack, inches from her hands. "You're so beautiful and distracting. Could you maybe change so we can go somewhere and talk?"

"*Coño.* The things you say." He gripped her waist tighter. "I love your honesty. And your hands. And especially your lips. That kiss." He stared at her mouth and groaned. "But you keep pushing me away."

"I know. You're right." She stepped back. "That's why I'm here... that and for the instructional manual."

"The cunny book."

"I only have a few hours before I have to get back to Brynn, but I was hoping we could get to know each other a little better. To give you a better idea about why I..."

"Run?" He cocked a brow.

"I'd call it disagreeing. But I swear, I'm usually the most easy-going of all my friends. I never have conflict or arguments."

"Boring."

"What?" She laughed even as she gave him space. She should be annoyed, but he looked so sincere she couldn't muster up the indignation. "Are you calling me boring?"

"You? Boring? Never." He stood to get closer, crowding her in. "How are you supposed to learn anything, or share who you are, if you don't argue a little?"

"I never thought about it that way. I usually give in—that's the approach that's worked for me so far."

"But you won't give in to me?" He put his hands on his hips, emphasizing the deep V cutting though his waist and angling toward his hips. So gorgeous. "Reina?"

Her eyes snapped up to his, and his frown eased somewhat.

"See something you like?"

Her eyes went wide as she smiled, unable to keep things from him when he asked a direct question. She nodded but resisted the urge to pinch herself to focus. This was important. "I want to talk."

"About the class?" He looked away.

Is he having second thoughts? "About us."

"Us?" He straightened, his mouth kicked up at the side with his now familiar dangerous grin. Dangerous because of what it did to her body. "Stay right there."

"Are you changing?" She should look away, but she was fascinated as he grabbed nylon sweats from his locker and pulled them on under the towel. She held her breath, laser focusing on the thick bulge tenting the towel.

One lone thought crowded her addled brain: *Is it pierced too? Is it? Is it?*

"A-are we going to talk in here?"

"No. We can go to Alexei's office. He has a couch that he crashes on when things get busy." He grabbed a leather backpack, slammed the locker door shut, and indicated she should walk in front of him out of the locker room.

Only a few feet away was a spacious office with a large desk made out of light wood, a cream couch, and minimalist, cream furniture. The only splash of color was a small stained glass lamp perched in the corner of his desk. The greens and reds of the maple leaf design popped in the spotless office. "Alexei's so talented." Ren sighed. "This is nice. Super spacious. And *clean*."

The snick of the door locking made her spin around.

"Now we talk."

Chapter 14

TONGUE TRAP

THEO FELT AMPED. The same rush he felt when pushing himself to the limit on his bike or in the ring. Tonight felt like a challenge. In order to win this woman, he'd have to take the biggest leap of his life. It'd been years since he'd risked his heart. Countless one-night hook ups didn't count.

Reina is special. I need to convince her I'm worth it.

Coño, an hour ago he would never believe he'd be alone in a room with Reina. Ready to give up, he would have said goodbye to the only woman who'd piqued his interest since Rosie. It was a lonely prospect. Ren had taken up most of the extra space in his brain these past few months. He'd subsisted on fights, video games, and math theorems.

Otherwise, it was all Reina.

She'd exceeded every expectation: gorgeous, smart, funny, honest to a fault—she always shared how she felt, and the way she looked at him… *he couldn't get enough.* All the pent-up passion of the past few days tethered them together. Tonight, she wore a honey-colored wig which brought out the amber in her doe eyes.

She's here. I have my in. Don't fuck it up, Romero.

"You're locking the door?" she asked with a tilt to her head. Her hair brushed her shoulders, getting snagged on a cream scarf wrapped around her elegant neck. She wore a flowy black dress with burnt brown tights that caressed her shapely legs.

"No more interruptions." His voice came out gruffer than he intended. When she didn't move or put down her purse, Blue's words came back to him. *Don't scare her.* "Unless you want it unlocked?" He reached for the door.

"No. It's not that. I'm just nervous in general. I trust you." She looked around and set her stuff on Alexei's desk.

He froze, soaking in the nonchalant statement. It cost her so little, but it meant so much to him. *She trusts me.* Not wanting to give away how much that mattered, he cracked his knuckles and watched her. Again trying to figure her out. She wasn't scared, she was obviously attracted to him, so why did she keep running?

Maybe it's not about you, *pendejo.* Maybe it's about *her.*

"I'm sorry for all the confusion. Let's sit." She walked over to the sofa and grabbed one of the oversized pillows, setting it on her lap. Reina crossed one leg under her as she sat, patiently waiting for him to join her.

He wanted to drop to his knees and worship her with his mouth but she probably wasn't ready for that. *Woo her, fool.* He sat as close as possible without seeming stalkerish. But he craved proximity. Wanted an accidental touch, or to feel her minty breath on his cheek. Anything.

Again, she watched with an eager gaze, her eyes studying his bare chest. "Your tattoos are fascinating. I've never seen anyone with all black ink. It's so interesting because you use it as negative space—so the actual designs are your skin. So pretty..." She breathed. "Do they signify anything special?"

His cock went ramrod thick, begging for some attention from his queen. God, he loved her eyes on him. He could almost feel their touch. "They're mostly everything I love." Out of habit, he rubbed his palm over his heart. It was a rose, and its thorns grew and spread through every other design. It signified the beauty and pain connected to the most beautiful person he'd known.

"And these?" She ran her fingers down his arms.

He smiled, pulled from his reverie about the past. "Those are Gaussian ensembles, the most studied in RMT. These are what first got me interested in mathematical physics and probability theory."

"Why are you so interested in…what was it?"

"Random Matrix Theory." Normally, he'd never mention his field of study, but if it kept her here, in front of him where he could touch her, he'd do it. "It's basically a different way to look at the world. A deeper way. When I'm fascinated with something, I can get lost in it. For hours at a time."

"You're so smart." Reina sat quietly after that, studying him, and then zeroing in on his nipple piercings.

Fascinating. "What are you thinking right now?"

"Hmm?" she asked, obviously lost in thought as she stared at him.

"Reina?"

"Oh!" Her cheeks flushed a deep red and she smiled through the embarrassment. "I probably shouldn't say."

"Tell me," he growled, knowing in his gut it was something he wanted to hear, needed to know. He loved when she daydreamed, but only when he could tell she was thinking about him. "Give me something."

"I was thinking about how much I like to hear you talk math." She peeked at him between her lashes. "Also, I was wondering what those would feel like." She pointed at his piercings. "On my tongue."

"Jesus, Reina." He moved inches from her. "Do it."

"But we shouldn't."

"Why the hell not? And why'd you bring it up if you aren't going to do it?"

"Because you asked me! I didn't want to lie." She huffed. "It's not my fault you're so devastatingly sexy. Admit it, you did this on purpose."

"Did what?" Now he couldn't think beyond his throbbing cock.

She'd said she wanted to lick his nipples, and that he was sexy, and he was supposed to follow this conversation?

"Kept your shirt off to distract me." She sat up and untied her scarf. "Is it getting hot in here or is it me?" She held up her hand when he opened his mouth to answer. "Never mind. I came here to break the ice, to get to know each other so we could figure out what's happening between us."

"I know what's happening. I like you. I want to be with you. I want to help you with the class. Is that not clear?"

She opened her mouth and then shut it again. "You're so direct." She fanned her cheeks. "Why do I like that so much?"

Theo groaned and let his head drop back. "Everything you say turns me on, yet you're still way over there and I'm still thinking about you licking my nipples."

"I'm right next to you." She smiled.

"Not close enough," he complained.

"You're amazing." When he leaned in to snare her mouth, she placed her soft fingers over his lips. "Wait! I know our chemistry is intense, but it's important for me to get to know you a bit." She pulled her hand away, and he missed the warmth. "When I told Brynn about you volunteering to help me, she suggested we play an ice breaker game. That's what she and Alexei did."

"Alexie played games?" He scoffed. "I doubt it."

"He did. I think it's all about negotiating the class. I thought maybe we could play Two Truths and a Lie. I'll tell you three things about me, and you tell me which one is the lie."

He cocked a brow, highly suspicious of this game. Why couldn't they have a normal conversation? He'd listen to her talk all night. "And then you lick my piercings?"

Her eyes went wide, and she burst into laughter. "Yes, please." Her smile faded for a minute. "If you still want me to. My life is kind of complicated. Not for the faint of heart. You might not want to deal with all of it."

"I don't want—"

"*Please.* I'm a little nervous. I'm also a rule follower, and if that's how everyone else who taught the classes got to know each other, it must mean it works, right?" She tossed her hair over her shoulder. "And I'd really like this to work."

Me fucking too. "I'm in. As long as we're back to kissing and talking about me helping you teach the class."

"Why are you so obsessed with the class? I'm trying to get to know you."

"Because I've dreamed about making you come so hard you'll never…"

"Never what?" Her voice sounded breathy as she leaned in.

Damn fool. You're going to spook her. But he couldn't help himself. "You'll never forget me."

She blinked. "I could never forget you, Theo Romero." She shook her head. "Never."

Fuck. I'm a goner. To rein himself back in, because this stupid game was more important than his throbbing cock, he said, "Three things. Go."

"Uh, okay. I have a list somewhere…"

He growled in response.

"But I think I have a few memorized." She giggled, not put off by his impatience. "One, I grew up in Irvine, California. Two, I have dual citizenship, USA and Mexico. Three, I've never had a guy go down on me."

Wait, what? His mind couldn't process. Why would she bring up… was *that* the lie? Did he want that to be the lie? He had a shot at being the only one, but… should he talk about it?

He blurted out the first thing that came to mind. "Brynn said you were Mexican."

"I am." She smiled. "My mom was from Guadalajara, Mexico. Most people don't guess that because I take after my dad's side of the family."

She's a *guera.* No, she's a queen. "You didn't grow up in Irvine?" He didn't know what to wish for at this point.

"I did."

His chest ached. "The lie is that no one has ever gone down on you. Which means someone has." He shifted, his eyes narrowing. "You seriously want me to talk about you *with other guys*?" His voice increased with each word.

"You get mad so quickly. That's cute." She brushed a lock of his hair off his forehead. "I have had someone... do *it* to me." She cleared her throat and looked away. "But the reason I brought it up is because it was only one time and it was awful."

His body tensed. "What happened?"

"We were young, and I'd never done it, and he hadn't either. It was uncomfortable for both of us, and he wasn't happy about it." She twisted her fingers in her lap.

"What did he say?" he asked through clenched teeth.

"Um... you know, stuff like it was taking too long." Her voice dropped to a whisper. "And about how it looked. So that's been my only experience with it."

"I'll kill him." He cracked all of his knuckles. Left hand, right hand. Then he cracked them all over again. "Tell me who it is."

"No! No." She scooched forward and placed her hands over his. "No murdering, please. I shared so you would understand why I don't want your help with the class. Brynn said she's done all the research and even though it won't be comfortable, I can wing it up there."

His mind spun. For once in his life, he was speechless. He stared at her for a lifetime.

"Can't we get to know each other? And take that off the table?" She shrugged. "It's not for everybody." When he didn't answer, she asked, "Are you okay?"

"No, I'm not fucking okay." He exploded into action and went to his knees in front of her. "I'm not going to let that asshole's words be the last ones you think about when somebody goes down on you."

"S-somebody?"

"Not somebody. Me! I'm going to devour you for however long it takes. Hours. Months. There's no taking *too long* if you're feeling good."

"There isn't?"

He kneaded her thighs through her tights, spreading her legs wide and leaning in so her beautiful full breasts pressed against his chest. "I want to help you teach the class. But more importantly, I want to help you conquer this misconception."

"But we're playing a get-to-know-you game." Her breath hitched as his hands traveled an inch higher above her knees.

"Fine. One, I'm Cuban. Two, I'm a fighter. Three, I don't want to eat your pussy for days, and lick all the liquid heat coating your plump lips." His hands inched higher. "Guess which one is the lie."

"*Omigosh.* Devastatingly sexy," she whispered and spread her legs an inch wider. Then she sat up straight and grabbed his shoulders, but she pulled him closer instead of pushing him away. "But there's still so much I have to tell you, explain to you about my life. I—"

"You said you weren't hooking up with anyone."

"I told you I wasn't!" She cupped his cheeks and his eyes closed for a brief second. "I haven't for a long time."

He groaned but kept himself still. "Will you give us a chance, get to know me, and see if this works?" He slid his hands up until he cupped her right where her legs fit into her hips. "No more slamming the door in my face?"

"I didn't slam—"

"*Reina.*"

"Yes, yes. I promise. But I'm really nervous about you going down on me. Scoot back, give me a minute to think." She asked for space but still gripped his shoulders tight.

"As soon as you let me go. I'll stop." He kneaded her thighs harder.

"I can't think."

He stilled his hands.

"No, don't stop. That feels so good," she whimpered.

Love her sweet words. He wanted to drive her to the edge. "Now picture my hands between your legs, my mouth on your plump clit. Are you wet for me, Reina?"

"Oh God, *yes*. Okay, okay... I'll do it, but I have a few stipulations."

"*What?*"

"You know I only think it's sexier when you get growly."

"Reina."

"Okay." She jumped when his thumb brushed against her throbbing core. "We can do this if maybe we start slowly? Above the clothes?"

He pretended to contemplate the offer. He'd take anything he could get. "Yes."

She placed her hands on top of his. "One more thing."

"Is this the *last* thing?" He was about to explode.

She giggled and shrugged. "Maybe? I think so. But this is important."

"What?"

"Since this is about the class..." She gripped his forearms as if to gather her courage, her creamy skin tomato red as she continued, "I want to use the manual."

"The one with instructions for the class?" He didn't even know how to process this request. He wanted to devour her and she wanted to...read? "While we're messing around?"

She nodded.

"Let me make sure I understand. I will be going down on you but..."

"Over the clothes."

"Over the clothes—and you'll be reading the techniques?"

"Out loud." Her eyes fluttered shut as he massaged her shapely thighs.

Fuck it. Why not? He threw back his head and laughed. "Go get your instruction manual."

Chapter 15

LICKING THE BEAN

"LET ME UP to get the book."

"No, you stay there. I'll get it." He pointed at her, super grumbly and sporting a thunderous frown. Her favorite. "Don't move an inch. Nothing's going to interrupt us this time."

Ren felt his absence when he rose, reality creeping in, so she sat up, and snapped her legs closed.

"I gave you one simple instruction. Not to move. And look what you did." He threw the manual on her lap and fitted between her legs again. "I can feel your complicated mind churning. Stop thinking."

"Not possible." But his warmth went a long way in relaxing her.

"Kiss me."

"Yes, please." She met him halfway, her hands fisting his dark hair as he slowly nuzzled her neck, his short beard abrading her cheek. Shivers exploded down her spine. He nibbled at her jaw and pressed his pillow lips against hers, just a deep caress, peppering and nudging hers open. This kiss was the antithesis of their first one. That had been angry heat, this was a slow burn. He was coaxing her into trusting him.

He worked her mouth, cupping her cheek and tilting her jaw at the perfect angle. "I love your lips." He continued down her throat toward her sensitive breasts. "But I'm obsessed with these." He skimmed her chest, biting her shirt buttons with his teeth. "I would cut off my right hand to see these beautiful breasts. Do you know how many times I got off from the idea of sucking your nipples? What color are they? How do they feel? Taste?"

"My nipples are light brown. They're really soft." She couldn't resist torturing him, she knew the DDs were her best feature, looking particularly impressive because of her height. "I've never tasted them, but now I'm thinking I should."

He groaned. "If I was ever lucky enough to see that, I'd die a happy man." He opened his mouth and swallowed a pert areola through her shirt.

"Oh, my God!" This man. His talent. His *pierced tongue*. "That feels incredible."

His big hands cupped her thighs again, massaging from knee to hip, creating delicious friction as his mouth devoured her other breast.

Is it possible to come from over-the-shirt, boob action?

"I want to feel you." He sucked in a breath, breathing her in. "Lick your skin and taste you."

He continued to massage her thighs, and Ren wondered how much better his hands would feel against her bare skin. "Take them off."

He smirked.

"But that's it!"

Theo reached up to the waist of her tights and had them down in one pull. They snagged on her boots. "Theo!"

"What?" He tossed off one of her shoes and then the other. "I had to move fast in case you changed your mind." His hands clamped against her tense muscles and moved in that long, deep caress.

"Oh, dear God." She never knew her legs were so sensitive.

"You better start reading or else I'm going in on my own."

Read? "That's right. The manual!" She fumbled with the notebook and managed to open it to page one as he licked his way up her inner thigh. "Everyone has a smell," she read aloud. That didn't sound sexy. *At all.* What kind of manual was this? "Um, that was weird."

"Weird? Let me check." He dove down and put his face in her crotch. "Hell yeah, you smell."

"What?"

"*Tremenda manguita.* Sexiest smell ever." He rubbed his face against her thigh. "Might make me come in my pants."

Her body tensed up again as he raised her skirt. The only thing between her vagina and his pierced tongue were white lace panties. "That feels amazing." Her eyes fluttered shut, but then she rallied. "Need to keep reading."

"No, you don't."

"Everyone has a taste," she read, ignoring his protest. Oh God. Why had that been the next line?

He kissed his way from her thighs to her core. "Want to taste you so bad." He opened his big mouth, his tongue ring glinting off the low light, and devoured her through her panties. Her whole body clenched. Over and over he worked her with his tongue. "Let me, Reina. Let me taste you." His hands inched toward her panties.

"I haven't read any of the techniques."

"Read them, and I'll do them." He sat up. "Tell me this won't feel even better on your bare skin."

No, I can't lie. She cupped his face and kissed him with all her pent up passion. But even while she feasted on him, she felt like a coward, afraid to let go. The old memories held weight.

He pulled back and growled when she didn't tell him what he wanted to hear. "Keep reading."

"It asks, 'Should you write the alphabet with your tongue?'"

"Should I?" He sat up, his hair standing on end.

"Nope! Trick question." She panted as she read, "It says here that most women need a consistent and slow touch to orgasm—so that's a *no bueno*."

"Got it." He returned to licking her through a small patch of fabric. "Reina, all I'd have to do is push your panties to the side, and I'm licking you." He growled. "It would feel so good."

"*Omigod.* Just keep doing it the way we agreed. Please." *Why aren't I brave enough to say yes?* The whole experience was a giant mind fuck. Just as she barreled headlong into an orgasm, her ex's words would float through her head. Vividly, she recalled him laughing and wiping his mouth in disgust.

So she kept reading, trying to block out the negativity and get out of her head. "It says it usually takes women twenty-five to forty minutes to finish! You see? That's a really long time. What if I'm someone who takes even longer?"

"There is no *too long.*" He licked long and slow, nuzzling her clit and making her jump. "Don't you get it?"

He says that now.

Theo moaned against her core, the rush of air tickling her soaked vulva, vibrating the sensitive tissue with just the right touch. She clamped down hard but couldn't reach release. "*That...* do that again." Even without a full release, she knew this was the best sexual experience of her life.

"You're not reading."

She fumbled for the book. "It says to make eye contact."

His eyes swung up to hers, and it might be the sexiest thing she'd ever seen.

"Vary the pacing," she read. "The clitoris needs constant slow contact, but overstimulation is possible."

The man had a talented tongue. He swirled, he licked, he thrust, and then he used his tongue piercing and her pleasure spiked. "You're so talented," she babbled. "So good. So good!"

"Yes, Reina. This is how it'll always be." He didn't come up for air, just continued with the measured, slow licks.

"I'm supposed to be reading." She wanted to sob with the growing pressure that kept leveling off instead of taking her over the edge. "I want to come *so bad.*"

"Then let me touch you! I'll rip your panties off in seconds, Reina."

"I want to." Ren sat up on her elbows, her eyes going wide when she watched his tongue working her over. *So sexy.* "But…"

His head snapped up, and his eyes narrowed. Always suspicious. "But *what?*"

"I'm having a hard time concentrating because it's intense and I feel…I don't know. Watched."

"Of course, I'm watching you." His gaze fell. "I'm watching every dripping inch of you. I can't get enough. Look, you soaked your panties through."

"I did? Lemme see." She leaned forward. "You find that sexy? It's not gross?"

"Reina." His thunderous frown eased, and he cupped her jaw. "I love it because it means you want me. That's so sexy. That and your breasts. I can't stop thinking about them, and I haven't even seen them yet." He kissed her gently and that may have been the biggest turn on of all. "Maybe a different position would help."

"Oh my God…" she scrambled for the book, "you're brilliant."

"I swear to God, I'm going to rip that book in half."

"No, don't do that. It talks about facesitting. When a women straddles a man's face while he's lying down." Ren's whole body thrummed with excitement. If she didn't have to worry about him watching, if she could feel a little more in control… it might work. "Can we do that?"

"Hell *yeah.* You want that?" He stood and scooped her up in his arms. "But no panties."

She brushed his hair back from his forehead and smiled. He licked his lips, and she kissed him with every ounce of passion coursing through her body. "I want that too. Your tongue, my bare skin."

They both moaned.

In seconds, he was laying on the couch and she straddled his face.

"Wait. I need to take off my—"

RIIIIPPPP! He tore her panties off with one tug and dove inside her entrance with his tongue.

The feel of his wet mouth lapping her up, coating every inch of her soaked lips, made her zone out, the pleasure was so intense. Blissed out on desire, she relaxed and took her time. She enjoyed the freedom to set the pace, the manual tossed across the room.

This man, with the talented tongue and piercing, went to *town*. "Pinch your nipples."

"You love my boobs." She hefted them up through her shirt and scissored both nipples between her fingers, her back arching in pleasure. They'd always been extremely sensitive.

"Fuck yeah, I love that. Keep pinching them. So good! I about to finish before you do." He adjusted himself and she was almost knocked off balance.

Is he tugging down his sweats? Ren strained to look back over her shoulder. "I want to see."

"Of course you do. So fucking sexy. Love your pretty mouth." He groaned. "Can feel it. I'm about to explode!"

Her eyes fluttered shut and felt close, *so close*, to coming. His thick tongue coasted long and slow, over and over, taking her to the edge.

"Keep moving. Like that." His warm breath washed over her. He penetrated her entrance with his finger, and breached her tight entrance to stimulate her G-spot.

"Yes, yes, *yes!*" Her orgasm barreled through her, and she rode it long and hard. Her inner walls clamped down so hard, she gripped the arm of the couch for balance. Never in her life had she experienced such pleasure, and his talented tongue never stopped, extending and prolonging the intensity. She couldn't look back, could only go along for the ride. She imagined him squeezing his cock, faster and faster.

He clamped his hands on her thighs and shouted, "Right there with you!"

Chapter 16

SLURPIE

WEDNESDAY

"HOW ARE YOU feeling?" Ren popped her head through the den door, peeking in on Brynn. It had been a long day at the hospital. Her bones ached, but she couldn't wait to check in on her friend.

"Bored out of my mind. Come in, please. Tell me everything about what happened yesterday with you and Theo. I must have fallen asleep by the time you came home last night." Brynn tapped the bed. The Calvo stunner looked lovely in a light-blue sweat suit.

"Yeah, I put in a twelve hour shift." Ren closed the door behind her and sat on the bed, facing her smiling friend. "You look so much better today."

"I feel better. Thanks. You look exhausted." She brushed her bangs out of her face. "I'd get you some tea, but I'm not allowed to get up."

"That's okay. I can get it myself in a bit."

"Tell me, please. I was so worried about how it went. I'm hoping you have good news so I can live vicariously through you and your new hot, but grumpy, boyfriend."

"He's not my boyfriend." She pressed her hands to her warm cheeks. "But he's definitely hot." She giggled.

"You look scandalized. I love it. Spill the tea. Did the ice breaker work?"

"Not really, he mostly wanted to talk and convince me to…"

"What?"

"Ride his face like a hardcore cowgirl!"

"You didn't," she shrieked.

"I did!"

The two of them doubled over in laughter, randomly yelling out things like, "Ride 'em cowboy" and "Giddy yup." Eventually they settled, both sprawled out on the bed.

"Oh my gosh, that is so exciting. I can't believe you went for it."

"I did. I tried to use the manual but then it all felt so good that it got tossed. Not that he needed any instruction."

"A man with a tongue piercing better know what to do with it, if you know what I mean." Brynn cleaned her glasses on her sweatshirt. "Did you get a chance to talk about all the other stuff too? About Nicholas?"

"Nope. I was too busy."

They started squealing all over again.

"Sounds like a whole lot of fun in there." Ms. Hattie pushed on the door, her smile a mile wide. She was the infamous leader of The Ladies that Lunch. The group of octogenarians that helped run the school now that Ms. Belle had passed. "Are you working up my baby girl, Ms. Ren? She's supposed to be resting."

"Ms. Hattie." Ren hopped off the bed and was enveloped in a Jean Nate scented hug. "What are you doing here? I thought you and The Ladies already left."

"We're having a sleepover tonight. Ms. Scarlett and Henry, Ms. Babe and Ms. Nancy—they'll all be here soon. We're having a movie night with Brynn."

"How fun. What are you going to watch?"

"Anything with that Jason Momoa. He reminds me so much of my Henry." Ms. Scarlett, decked out in her signature pink outfit walked into the room with her boyfriend Henry, who didn't exactly scream Jason Momoa. He was tall, thin, slightly stooped, and looking every day of his ninety years. Scarlett was a spry eighty and loved everything pink. The two were inseparable and still quite active, according to Ms. Scarlett who took TMI to a new level.

Ren greeted each of them with a hug and a peck on the cheek, always so filled with warmth when she was with them. She hadn't grown up around much family, so seeing them always felt like coming home.

"That means you're free to go out with your bucking bronco," Brynn whispered and winked.

"Who's that?" Ms. Hattie could smell gossip. As Ren's mother would say, Ms. Hattie was, "All in the *masa.*"

"Ren's been dating Theo, Ms. Hattie."

"I wouldn't call it dating—"

"Oh, my. Theo? So smart and intense, that one. Such a sweet boy."

"He really can be. When he's not bossing me around. But even then it's sweet somehow." If Ms. Hattie could see beneath his gruff exterior, Ren knew her instincts were right on track.

"Yes." Ms. Scarlett patted Old Henry's arm. "We seriously considered inviting him into our," she looked at Hattie, "what did Dacey call it…a *throttle?*"

"No, that can't be right." Ms. Hattie put her hands on her hips. "What *was* it called?"

"Henry, what was it?" Old Henry was shuffling over to the seat in the corner and didn't appear to hear her. "Well, needless to say, before I realized how desperately jealous and ferocious Henry felt about me, we considered inviting a third man to join us."

Ren's mouth dropped open, but she couldn't produce sound.

She also refused to look at Brynn, in case she lost it. A *throuple*? Was that what Ms. Scarlett was talking about?

"I had plans to announce it during Dacey's class. Not with Theo, of course, but a nice gentleman I had met on the computer." Ms. Scarlett placed a hand against her chest, clearly in the heat of the juiciest parts of her story. "But I couldn't do it. Not after I saw how it affected Henry. I would never want to devastate him like that."

Ren looked to Henry, who had nodded off, his head thrown back as he gently snored. "That's very considerate of you, Ms. Scarlett."

"Yes, it was. We were also worried about engaging with someone who frequents the school. I wouldn't want him to fall in love with me, and then I'd have to let him down gently. Henry is the man of my heart."

Henry startled awake and grabbed Ms. Scarlett's hand and kissed it.

"Of course." Ren's heart melted. *That's true love.* She hid her smile behind her hand and contemplated how Theo would react when she told him the news.

I can't wait.

"If we can't have him, we're so happy you can." Ms. Scarlett swept out a dramatic hand.

"Thank you?" Ren looked to Brynn, who was hiding *under* the covers, her whole body shaking.

"*Hermanas?*" Twin voices floated through the door.

"That must be Ms. Babe and Ms. Nancy." Ms. Hattie clapped her hands. "In the back room! I'll come get you." She looked at Ren. "Baby, will you help me bring in some more chairs, we're going to join Brynn in here. Oh, and maybe you can help me with this projector my grandson gave me. I haven't taken it out of the box but apparently you can attach your phone somehow and watch the movie on a wall."

"Absolutely, Ms. Hattie. I have one of those. They're great. You can probably watch it on that blank wall there." She pointed at the wall directly across from Brynn.

Ms. Hattie greeted Nancy and Babe, the telenovela watching sisters who loved to wear matching track suits. After saying hello, Ren walked into the ballroom to find the folding chairs and pillows. Her phone rang.

"You home from work?" Theo's gruff voice danced along her spine. He always checked in, texting or calling throughout the day. She knew it came from a deeper place of worry, so it hadn't bothered her so far.

"Yup. I'm at the charm school. Actually, it turns out I'm free tonight. What are you doing?"

"I might be free."

"Hold on." Ren grabbed the chair and hauled it over to the den, leaning it against the wall as she tucked her phone between her shoulder and cheek. She was halfway through the ballroom to get the second chair when the doorbell rang. "Oh shoot, now I have to get the door."

"I'll wait."

Ren dragged the folding chair with her and pulled open the wide front door. "Theo!" She gasped. "What're you doing here?" She spoke into the phone and to him simultaneously.

"*Mi Reina.* Did you miss me?" He scooped her up and kissed her within an inch of her life. "Wanna come to a *quinceañera* with me?"

"On a Wednesday night?" She peppered his pillow lips with kisses because she couldn't help herself.

"It's a rehearsal dinner. There'll be music and booze, and a bunch of annoying fifteen-year-olds. But we can ignore them." He leaned in closer. "Why'd you stop kissing me?"

"Because you were speaking."

"Don't stop."

She giggled and licked at his lips, her entire body going loose at his low groan.

"Hello there, young man." Ms. Scarlett caught them, with Ren smothering him with kisses and her feet dangling in the air. He hadn't put her down, and she loved it. Ms. Scarlett didn't even blink. "I'll tell Henry you're here. He'll be thrilled."

"Okay?" Theo frowned and looked at Ren. "What's that about?"

Ren burst into laughter. "You missed out on an opportunity of a lifetime." When he cocked a brow, she laughed harder. "I'll explain later. Put me down."

"No."

"Why not?"

"I like you in my arms."

It was a miracle her panties didn't drop to the floor. This guy. He even said it with a frown, and it still turned her on. "What should I wear?" She brushed his hair back from his forehead. It was longer from when she'd first seen him so many months before, and she liked it, a lot.

"You look perfect. Like always."

"Thanks." For that he got another quick kiss. "Okay, but you're going to have to put me down because The Ladies and Old Henry need us to bring some chairs into Brynn's room. They're going to do a movie night."

Theo set her down and had the projector up in minutes. The movie crew was happy as clams as they watched the show and munched on popcorn.

Chapter 17

JEWEL MUNCHING

"I'VE GOT A surprise for you." Theo took her by the hand, walking backward to the parking lot at the back of the school.

"What?" Ren stopped dead in her tracks when she saw him palm a helmet hanging from the biggest motorcycle she'd ever seen.

"It's a Ducati Monster. My baby. Thought you two should meet."

She froze, the world around her fading for a minute, her only point of reference was her heart slamming into her chest, beating an erratic thump between her ears. She couldn't breathe.

"Hey, *hey*. Reina, are you okay?" Theo cupped her face and tilted her chin so she could look into his eyes. "It's okay. I'm here. Look at me. Breathe."

"Breathe," she repeated and lifted a shaky hand, wanting to say she was okay, but knew she wasn't. A motorcycle. *He rides a motorcycle.* How had she forgotten that? One of the many reasons she'd originally avoided dating him.

"Is it the bike? Are you freaked out? We don't have to take it."

She focused on her lungs, her breathing—the mini panic attack a surprise. It had been several years since she'd had one, and they never got easier. She clung to his forearm, and his strong hands settled on her shoulders, kneading the tight muscles. "I'm sorry."

"Come sit down." He led her to the school's steps. She sat at the top, he sat one below, bringing them eye to eye. "What happened?"

"It was nothing." She waved it away weakly. "I get overwhelmed sometimes."

"It wasn't *nothing*. Don't shut me out. I hate that."

She gazed into his intense stare; the angry expression should have sent her running, but she loved it. Because she knew he was mad *for* her.

"I lost somebody... on a bike. A long time ago. And I haven't been able to ride one since. I don't even like to go near them."

"You haven't been on one recently? Does that mean you used to ride?"

"Yeah. I loved it. Before it destroyed my life."

"Can I ask how the accident happened?"

"My ex-boyfriend went up into the hills. I guess he switched motorcycles with a friend, but his bike was a lot more powerful than my ex was used to. Somehow, he forgot his helmet or didn't want to wear one and... he lost control. He slammed into the mountain."

"I'm sorry, Reina. Come here." He hauled her into his arms and rocked her for a while. "He was reckless."

"What? He..." She squeezed her eyes shut, his direct tone speaking to a part of her she hadn't been able to acknowledge. Nicholas *had* been reckless about so many things. He was young and beautiful and so full of life. But also impulsive, at times. "Yes, he was."

It simultaneously broke her and healed her to admit that.

"Riding motorcycles is dangerous. But that's why you have to be careful. Wear the proper gear, take your time."

"Are you reckless, Theo?"

He looked down, scuffing his boot against the step. "I would never be careless with you. I promise."

But that didn't mean he hadn't been reckless with himself. The fighting, the riding... She didn't want another man who played fast and loose with his life. But she had no right to ask him to change. They'd been on one date. Not even. They'd hooked-up once. But she could listen and try to be honest with her feelings.

"That worries me. It's not only about the motorcycle. It's about the underground fighting, too. I don't want you to get hurt. Brynn told me the story about what you had to do to get Alexei out. Will you have to hurt yourself to stop fighting?"

"Nope." He grinned. "I can stop whenever I want to."

"What? How?"

"My family is what you'd call... diverse. We have police officers, lawyers—hell, my cousin is a DA."

"And they let you fight?"

"I wasn't finished. I also have gang bangers and a few highly connected members in *la mafia*. We have struck a tentative balance in the family, but it gives me the freedom to go in or out. No one will touch me."

"Two sides of the same coin. Wow. Then why would you do something so dangerous?" She punched him on the shoulder and then immediately soothed the area with her hand.

"I lost someone, too." He cleared his throat. "Sometimes you need a little distraction to get through the day. Plus, I'm good at fighting. The best."

"I have no right to ask you to change, but I want to be with someone who takes care of himself as much as he takes care of me. I can't go through that again. I lost too much."

"So you hide and never take chances? You've cut yourself off from the world."

Is that what I've been doing? "So you make reckless choices, and I cut myself off from the world. We're both seriously messed up." She kissed him because she couldn't help herself.

His arms banded around her and a simple peck became a make-out session. "Love kissing you."

Eventually, she pulled back, slowing things down until she ended it with one last nip of his full bottom lip. "You're the best kisser ever."

"I am. Don't forget it." He stood and held out his hand. "We can take your car. I'll drive."

"No, you won't." Had she cut herself off from something she enjoyed, like so many other parts of her life? People rode motorcycles every day. It didn't mean all of them ended in an accident. "Maybe I could try?"

He stepped forward and traced her cheek. "My brave, queen. You sure?"

Her hands shook as they walked over. She rubbed her sweaty palms together and stood rooted to the spot. "Why is it so big?"

"Because it's the best." He laughed until he saw her face. "How about we start small? Sit on the bike."

"Sit, he says," she repeated, not sure if her leg would reach that high.

"I'll help you."

"But I don't want to get on alone. If we rode, it would be together, right?"

"I like that." His playful smile was back. "I'll put you on, and I'll slide in front of you, okay?" He grasped her waist and waited until she nodded, easily lifting her onto the massive bike.

She grasped the seat, unsure of her balance because her feet didn't touch the ground. *Short girl problems.*

Theo quickly joined, balancing the bike with his long legs.

His thick thighs bunched as he steadied the bike, making her sigh. Leaning into him, she wrapped her arms around his middle. Ren snuggled into him, his leather jacket suffused with his musk and heat. It made her feel safe. As long as they didn't move. "This is... nice."

"What you doing with those hands, Reina?"

"Nothing." Her palms may have slipped under his button-down

shirt. She gasped when she felt the dip and curve of his shredded stomach. The man was a masterpiece, and she couldn't get enough.

"Don't start something you won't finish."

Who said she wouldn't—

Theo revved the massive bike, and Ren screamed. Right in his ear.

"Ow! That was loud."

"I said I wanted to *sit* on the bike. That's it." Ren thumped him on the shoulder. "We don't even have helmets on! You said you weren't reckless." She pulled back and looked around, trying to figure out the best way to dismount this beast. "Let me down!"

He grasped her hands. "I said I would never put you in danger, and I meant it. This is baby steps. I wanted you to feel the power of the bike. I would never take off without telling you. And I always wear a helmet. Period."

She pursed her lips but went back to hugging his back when she felt the truth of his words. It felt good to hug him. It even felt good to yell at him sometimes. She never got to yell at anyone.

"Do you feel the power of the engine? How it rumbles between your thighs?" He looked back at her and smirked. "One of my favorite places to be."

She laughed and hid her face in his jacket.

"I like you with me. How does it feel?"

Memories of the wind in her hair, as she'd flown down the 405 freeway in high school, assailed her. It had been exhilarating. And even though it was mixed with some healthy terror, she wanted to conquer at least one small fear. "Do you think... we could go around the block? But that's it?" She rushed on.

"Hell yeah. I'm so proud of you. I'll take care of you. Always." He winked and handed her an extra helmet, slowly inching out of the parking lot. "Hold on. I've got you."

And he did, treating her as delicately as spun glass as they carefully navigated their way through Ms. Belle's tree-lined, neighborhood.

Chapter 18

MUFF DIVING

REN LOOKED OUT the passenger side window—yes, Theo had won the argument and was driving her car—studying his parents' neighborhood in El Sereno. She'd only worked at White Memorial Hospital a short time and was slowly getting to know the surrounding East Los Angeles neighborhoods. The densely packed houses scattered over steep hills were charming.

"Here we are." Theo parked the car in a root filled driveway, the small stucco home surrounded by avocado trees. "Listen, before we go in, I want to tell you about my family. They are absolutely *crazy*. So if you feel overwhelmed—"

"Teófilo*! Mi amor!*" A tiny dark-haired woman flung open the driver's side door and peppered Theo with kisses. "Where have you been? The *quince* practice started an hour ago."

"Ma, stop." He got out of the car and hugged her. When Ren joined him, he grabbed his mom's hand and turned her toward Ren. "I went to pick up a friend."

"*Ay, que bonita. Me llamo,* Julieta." She threw her arms around Ren and kissed her cheek. "*Hablas español?*"

"*Un poquito, pero no hablo bien.*" She'd told them she didn't speak Spanish, but responded in kind. "*But I understand most of it.*"

Theo and his mom spoke in rapid fire Spanish. Ren caught most of it and heard Theo share her name. His mother, Julieta, kept repeating Ren as if the three letter word didn't make sense. Eventually, she turned to Ren in disbelief and asked her for her name *again*. To make it easier she replied, "Adrenilda."

An older man, slender and quite spry, stepped up to them. "You poor girl. Your mother named you *that*?"

"*Tío*, that's not cool." Theo took Ren's hand. "Meet my Uncle Hugo."

"What kind of name is Adrenilda?" his mother asked Ren with a smile, switching to English flawlessly.

"I think it's German. It was my grandmother's name, on my father's side. He was German and Polish."

"That explains it. Family names. They're the worst, no?" *Tío* Hugo kissed Ren's cheek in greeting. "Is that what you call her, nephew? Adrenilda?" he shuddered.

"I call her Reina."

Tío Hugo took her measure, staring a few seconds too long. "It fits."

Theo's mom and *Tío* Hugo led them to a huge backyard surrounded by a wrought iron fence. On one side was an open-ended tent with foldout tables. The other side was grass—where a group of about twenty or so teenagers danced and pushed each other around.

Tío Hugo called out to the crowd of teens and guests, "*Oye!* Meet Reina. Teófilo's *reina*." *Tío* clapped in delight, and all the kids openly laughed and pointed at Theo.

Theo rolled his eyes and ignored them.

Ren's cheeks felt molten lava hot.

"Sit. Sit." His mother brushed back Ren's hair, and she was immediately self-conscious. Even though she shouldn't be, she was relieved she wore her Margarita wig, the one that looked the most like her own hair. Wigs and the Latinx community were tricky. So much identity went into hair, and women of a certain generation sometimes were scandalized by obvious wigs.

Like Nicholas' mother.

"Beautiful." Julieta patted Ren's shoulder and kissed Theo again. She went down the table, greeting all of the other guests.

"You're so lucky. I love your mom." Ren leaned into Theo and added, "I think *El Cubano*, badass fighter, might be a mama's boy."

"No, I'm not," he grumbled.

"Are you hungry? I'll let you eat before those *chamacos* eat all the food." They sat at a foldout table toward the back of the yard. She and Theo had a perfect view of all the teenagers dancing and goofing around in preparation for the *quince*. The traditional waltz music cued up, and they all rushed into place.

"I have to ask." *Tío* Hugo leaned his chin on his hands. "What *are* you?" He eyed her hair and studied her face.

"That's rude, *hermano*." Theo's mom admonished him. "You need to soften your approach. Not everyone is as nosy as you."

"How can it be rude to ask where someone is from?"

"That's not how you said it." Theo slung an arm over Ren's shoulders.

"It's okay." Ren was already fascinated with Theo's uncle. She gravitated toward people who were unapologetically themselves. Clearly, this man did and said whatever he wanted. What must that feel like? She glanced at Theo with his heavy arm draped around her shoulders and realized, like uncle, like nephew. "As I told Señora Julietta, my mom was originally from Mexico and my dad was Polish."

"Was?"

"Yes, she died when I was young, around six. And my dad died a few years back." It had been a one-two punch between Nicholas's accident and her dad's death. He'd been sick a long time, but she'd never thought she would lose her ex-boyfriend in the same week. Her mom's death, well… that was a rusty ache that never abated.

"How is it your pronunciation is so perfect, but you say you don't speak Spanish?" *Tío* Hugo asked, tilting his fedora just so, which gave him a debonair air he seemed to relish.

"Well, I used to only speak Spanish, but my mom died right before kindergarten started. I lived with my dad and we didn't have a big family, and he only knew how to speak English. I remember I was having such a hard time in school that he told me I would have to turn off my Spanish, like a light switch, so I could make room for English." She blinked out of the memory, temporarily sucked into one of the most difficult times in her life.

"I'm so sorry, Reina. To lose both your parents." Julietta came over and embraced both her and Theo, her warmth permeating the cold recollection of her parents' deaths. Ren's eyes watered, but she quickly blinked back the tears.

"I knew it." *Tío* Hugo slapped the table. "I can always tell, right, *hermana*? I always know a Latina. Not *Cubana* but since we live here, that's okay." He winked, eyeing his sister as if waiting for an explosion.

Theo's mom let loose, pointing out all the Mexican men *Tío* dated, how half their family was Mexican through marriage, including most of the kids at the *quince*. "We live in Los Angeles. What do you expect? You can't *say* these things!"

"He loves to tease her about that because after my dad died, she married a Mexican guy," Theo whispered in her ear, nuzzling her neck before pulling back. "He died, too."

"I'm sorry." Ren squeezed Theo's hand and watched the siblings fight, drinking it in. She'd always missed having a big family. It had just been her and her dad, along with her tía, a few times a year. Far too quickly that had been reduced down to her.

"You were married to a Mexican woman!" Theo's mother harrumphed, not quite finished with her tirade and walked away.

"Smartest thing I ever did. God rest her soul." *Tío* Hugo blew a kiss into the clouds. "She was so perfect; I never dated another woman again." He winked and took a deep drink of his beer.

Ren giggled and took a sip of the wine set in front of her.

"Tell me, Reina. What's a beautiful woman like you doing with this *pendejo*?"

Ren choked on her drink.

Theo growled. "*Tío. Carajo*, man. We go over this every time. Don't start with—"

"What? Tell me how I'm lying. He had his choice of schools, had a full scholarship to USC and what does he do? He fights. Throws it all away for the ring. He lets his beautiful brain get smashed in by losers. *Criminales*. I blame your *padre's* side of the family." He leaned in and whispered, "That's where we have all the troublemakers. Mark my words!" He slapped the table and looked around for confirmation. A few neighbors nodded and others groaned.

"I don't get smashed. I do the smashing." Theo scratched the side of his head, his tell when he was uncomfortable.

Theo's mom kicked his chair as she set overflowing plates of Cuban food on the table. *Rabo encendido* slathered in sauce, as steaming black beans and white rice overflowed on the plates.

"Oh my gosh, is this oxtail stew? That's my favorite!" Ren took a huge whiff, hoping for a change of topic.

The two were just getting started.

"You had it all and that's your response? You do the smashing? You see, he's already experiencing brain damage! You have experienced loss, yes. I understand that but we all have. You were very young, I know but... d*esmaya esa talla*. You must let it go."

"*Tío*. You won't even let me fin—"

"Enough! I've said my peace." *Tío* Hugo looked Ren over, his intent gaze resting on her scarf and finally ending on her wig. "Reina..."

Here it comes.

"Theo hasn't brought anyone home for a long, long time. You

must be special. Tell me about your wig," *Tío* Hugo asked, and pointed at her head with his fork.

"*Tío! Coño, carajo. Why would you ask her something like that?*" Theo thundered, far more upset on her behalf than his.

"What? I think they're beautiful." *Tío* Hugo chewed a bite and continued, "A few friends of mine perform at a club downtown, but some of their wigs look like *mierda*. Total shit. I can tell you got the expensive ones. Tell me everything."

Ren looked around and saw several of the guests not so discreetly waiting for her answer. Some stared openly at her hair, others looked anywhere but at her. A few shook their heads in sympathy.

"You're unbelievable." Theo stood and threw down his napkin. "I trust my family not to ask stupid-ass questions." He pointed at the group sitting next to them. "And you, mind your own business."

"Teófilo, calm down and stop yelling!" Theo's mom didn't even look up from across the yard as she shouted at him, continuing to talk to the guests.

"*Tío's* being a total ass, Ma."

"What did I do?" *Tío* threw down his own fork. "What? I asked a question."

"It's okay." Ren smiled and reached for Theo, touched he would be so offended on her behalf. But there was nothing wrong with *Tío* Hugo's honest question. As for the others, people always stared. She had no problem talking to those with a genuine interest. "I'm okay."

Theo glared one last time at the group next to them who suddenly became obsessed with their food. "I can't sit here with him. I'm getting another drink."

"Okay." Ren turned to *Tío* Hugo. "I'm super cheap, but I spare no expense when it comes to my hair." They had an in-depth conversation about the best wig shops in the city.

"Reina. Come here," Theo yelled from the end of the table, most of the guests having cleared out.

"Hmm?" Ren barely registered the question as she spoke to *Tío* Hugo, completely engrossed in his personal story about marrying his wife and realizing he was gay.

"That's fascinating." She patted his hand. "You're so brave. It's not easy to live your truth." She smiled. More than anyone, she understood how difficult it could be to show people the real you.

"Reina." Theo's warm hand on her shoulder knocked her out of her reverie. She blinked up at him. That always happened when she was engrossed in a story. She lost herself for a while. "You were supposed to join me."

"I'm coming right now."

"That was fifteen minutes ago."

"I'm sorry."

"Ignore that big baby. He wants all the attention to himself." *Tío* Hugo shoved more rice in his mouth.

"Why are you always giving me shit, *Tío*? What did I do? Accidentally kill your cat? I'm sick of the attitude." Theo slammed his drink on the table.

"I want you to live up to your potential!" *Tío* Hugo stood.

"You will behave at my house." Julietta set a few pieces of trés leches cake on the table, glaring at her brother and son until they both grumbled and sat. She then smiled at Ren as if nothing had happened. "Cake, Reina?" She rubbed her shoulder and kissed her on the cheek.

After Theo's mom found out Ren had lost her parents, she hadn't been able to stop comforting her. It was so thoughtful. Ren admired the way in which she handled her family.

Theo and *Tío* Hugo continued to murder each other with their eyes.

"That was amazing. How you handled those two." Ren leaned over and the petite woman leaned close. "Can you teach me how to do that?"

· "It's a gift." She winked. "But I have a feeling you might have it as well. If not, you better learn. My son is stubborn."

"*Gracias*, Julieta."

"Reina, I'm sure you can talk him out of this." *Tío* Hugo went back in on Theo the minute his sister had moved on and was out of earshot. Theo was momentarily distracted by one of the teens, who was trying to get him to dance.

It gave her a pit in her stomach, considering their conversation earlier. "I think you may have the wrong impression. Theo and I have only gone out once before tonight. I'm not his girlfriend. I don't have any right to tell him what to do."

"Do you hear what's she's saying, *sobrino*?" *Tío* Hugo said to his nephew. "She won't date someone who's associated with criminals. If you want her, you better stop fighting. She's worried sick." Tío winked at her.

Ren paused mid-bite. How had he gotten that from what she'd said? Not that she disagreed, but still. She looked at Theo's uncle and he winked at her, conspiratorially. "Um, no, wait... that's not exactly what I—"

"Would you?" Theo asked, his entire body tight with tension.

Ren was completely lost. "Would I, what?"

"Worry so much you couldn't be with me?"

She looked into his eyes and was sucked into his hazel gaze. Suddenly, the light-hearted conversation had turned into something serious. But she couldn't lie. "*Tío* Hugo's right. I would."

The rap music swelled, and all the dancers began twerking to Drake. They were practicing their signature dance, the show stopper they would perform after the traditional dances were complete. Ren forced a laugh, thankful for the distraction. Things were getting serious way too fast.

Chapter 19

CHERRY FLIP

THE EVENING WAS winding down. The dark of night surrounded the white tent. Someone set up a portable disco ball and the flashing lights created a festive glow. Theo dismissed his family and sat her far from the noise and teens. Most of the adults had left. Only a handful of diehard partiers remained.

"The rehearsal was so fun." Ren laughed. "I can't imagine how good the real thing will be."

"You have an open invitation. To any family event." He smirked. "They loved you. I think they like you better than me. At least, Tío Hugo does." His grin fell and a muscle in his cheek ticked.

"Thanks." Ren blinked, unexpectedly touched. She smoothed a finger between his brows.

Theo rubbed her arm. *El Cubano's love language is definitely touch.*

She ate it up. Couldn't get enough.

"Did my Tío Hugo embarrass you? With his questions?" Theo asked.

"About my wig?" Her eyebrows rose. "No. But how come you've never asked me about it?"

He paused, and she wondered if he'd prevaricate or pretend like he didn't know what she was talking about. Most people, in a bid to spare her feelings, feigned shock when she mentioned her wigs.

"If there was something to talk about, I figured you'd tell me when you're ready." He shrugged, his massive chest rising and falling in a sexy wave. "If we never talk about it, I'm okay with that too. You always look beautiful."

"You really mean that, don't you?" She felt the tug of a smile stretch across her face. This man floored her every time. "You're such a unique person. Anyone ever tell you that?"

He nodded. "All the time. But not in a nice way. Like you." He reached out and gently tugged the end of her brown curls but not enough to shift it.

Smart man. Someone taught him the right way to touch a woman's hair.

"I like it. Every time I see you it's a surprise." He looked down. "It's like when I get lost in Random Matrix Theory. I see more than the surface. I love to deep dive in theorems and equations." He blinked up at her. "That's the way it is with you. When you change your hair. It's the same to me. Always... you."

Ren opened her mouth and then shut it with a snap. Battling to own and embrace her Alopecia was a decades long battle. The fight to accept herself and not hide from the world had been deliberate and difficult, but so essential to her identity. But somehow, in a few simple words, Theo had rocked her world with his honesty and acceptance.

Which made her want to share her story. "Do you want to know why I wear them?" she asked softly, watching his face intently.

His entire frame tensed as he dropped the lock of her hair. Sitting back in his chair, he clenched his jaw and nodded.

She cocked her head to the side, fascinated by his reaction. He looked like he was prepping for the ring, or maybe bracing for impact. "This wig," she flicked the wayward lock over her shoulder, "looks a lot like my natural hair. Well, the way it used to look."

He ran his heavy-lidded gaze over her.

Shivering, she continued. "I always got a lot of compliments about my hair. No one knew where the curls came from. My mom had bone-straight-hair and my dad, well, he was bald, but even before that it wasn't curly." She smiled.

He nodded, his hands clenched into fists.

"A lot happened in a few short months, right at the beginning of college. I woke up with piles of it on my pillow. It only got worse from there." She sighed, lost in the fear and anxiety of that moment. "At first, I actually ignored it. Like I said, it was a crazy time so I didn't give it life. But soon I noticed bald spots, so my *tía* took me to the doctor."

He groaned and squeezed his eyes shut, running a big hand through his hair. He whispered to himself, like a chant.

"Hey." Ren cupped his cheek and his hazel eyes popped open. "Are you okay? What are you saying? I can't hear you."

"Reciting theorems. Centers my mind when I get overwhelmed." Theo grabbed her hand and squeezed tight. "I want you to be okay."

"You're worried I'm sick?"

He took in a few big gulps of air and looked like he might hyperventilate. He nodded.

"Oh my gosh, I'm so sorry." Ren popped up, nudging his stiff arms out of the way. She sat in his lap. "I'm fine. Look at me, gorgeous. I want you to listen, and hug me as tight as you want."

His thick arms banded around her and he squeezed her against him, surrounding her in his unique scent that reminded her of dusky nights and sin. He hugged her for a long time, his heaving chest eventually slowing.

"Do you want to talk about it?" She rubbed his back. This reaction was over the top and she knew it must be connected to his worry about hospitals.

"You talk first."

"*Por favor. No coman pan delante los pobres,*" one of the grandparents yelled over to them as they waved goodbye.

Ren smiled, familiar with the saying. It was one she'd heard from her tía. Roughly translated it meant, don't eat bread in front of the poor. Which was what people usually yelled at a couple who were making out. Not that they'd been kissing, but it probably looked like it.

Theo didn't laugh or smile, still shaken by their conversation. She understood his reaction even if she didn't know why, and had seen it many times before with her patients. Obviously, he'd experienced deep loss. His actions at the hospital and his worry about her health all led to one conclusion. He'd felt deep pain, and she found the best way to get through it was... to get through it.

"I'm going to tell you everything, and I want you to listen. So there are no secrets and nothing to worry about, okay?"

He shuddered and nodded, nuzzling her neck.

Her toes curled and heat bloomed between her legs, but she ignored it because this was about him, not her. "I have Alopecia Areata. Or just Alopecia. There are a few different kinds but mine primarily affects the hair on my head." She tried to lean back to see his reaction, but he held tight. "It's an autoimmune disease."

His head snapped back, and now he was looking her in the eye. He cupped her cheek and ran his thumb over her skin. "What does that mean?"

"For me, it means my hair falls out. Sometimes it grew back but eventually it fell out again. I tried so many treatments and procedures that never worked. With time, I gave up obsessing over every strand and shaved it all off. After that, I wore wigs."

"But I mean, are you okay? An autoimmune disease doesn't mean you're sick?"

"It means my immune system has sort of turned on itself. It doesn't always know who the bad guys are, and it went after my hair follicles. "But," she placed a finger over his lips so she could finish,

"I'm lucky."

"*What?*"

"I am. I don't have any of the other symptoms some people suffer with autoimmune disorders."

"You don't? Are you sure? I know I'm acting like a fucking wuss right now, but I'd want to know."

"You're not, and I'm telling you everything. To minimize symptoms, I try to eat as cleanly as possible, which is super hard because I *love* sweets. Like my trail mix but that doesn't count, right?" She laughed. "I sleep well, try and stay as stress free as possible, all the stuff most people should do anyway."

He shifted her closer.

"That's why I refused to make the hair thing a big deal. I see people in the hospital suffering far worse than me, although I let myself have a nice, long pity party at first. But once I shifted my perspective, I decided to be grateful about it."

"Grateful? For having a disease?"

"Yes, I choose gratitude, and I embrace how lucky I am. It could be so much worse."

"I never." He cleared his throat. "I never thought about it like that."

She looked down at his hands. So big and strong, looking invincible. But he hurt like everyone else. "It seems like you've experienced loss as well. If you ever want to talk about it, I'm here."

He sighed and loosened the steel band of arms around her torso. He sat back so they could see each other, maybe retreating the smallest bit. "Her name was Rosie. I met her when I was four years old, and I told everyone I knew that I would marry her one day. And I meant it."

Ren's body clenched in sympathy for Theo, because she guessed his story wouldn't have a happy ending. A tiny part of her also felt jealous because she'd grown greedy with him. Which she shook off immediately. *Not about you.*

"Alexei, Rosie, and I were inseparable until... we weren't. I didn't want to believe that Rosie was pulling away. Everyone told me I wore 'Rosie' colored glasses. But I believed in her. What's wrong with that?" He shook his head.

"Nothing. You loved her."

"I did. But she loved something more than me..." He sighed. "It's complicated." A few of the teens screamed out in laughter and Theo stiffened. "This isn't the best place to have this conversation, but if I don't do it now, I won't ever. I hate talking about it." His deep voice sounded like silk over sandpaper.

"If you want to stop—"

"She died in a house fire. The same fire that burned Alexei's legs." He took in shallow breaths and now she banded *her* arms around him. He crushed her to him. "I saw her... like that. In the hospital. It took her a few hours to die. It was the worst thing I've ever seen."

"I'm so sorry. I'm so sorry," she whispered like a chant, burrowing into him, sharing her support with touch. A long time passed before either could breathe properly again.

Theo sat back and ran his thumb under her eyes, brushing away the tears. "Let's go." The terror dropped from his eyes and his broad shoulders relaxed. "But first, kiss me, Reina. Let's eat some *pan*."

Chapter 20

CHOW DOWN

THEO FELT A thousand pounds lighter. He hadn't admitted, even to himself, that he worried about Reina and why she wore wigs. He loved everything about the way she looked, quirky clothes and wild hair, but he was relieved as hell that she was healthy.

Besides that, make-out sessions with the sexiest woman in the world always lifted his spirits. *I'm quickly becoming addicted to everything about her.*

"Be as quiet as possible," Theo whispered as he slowly moved her away from the tables.

"Why?" In typical fashion, Reina had lost her purse and was making a lot of noise as she searched around and under the table.

"That's not quiet." He grabbed her hand, the pressure in his chest easing. He wanted alone time, now. He'd dreamed of diving between her legs again, hearing her make those breathy sounds— feasting on those glistening lips. But if he didn't move quickly, the whole place would surround them to say goodbye, and that could take a half hour. "I'm trying to get out of here—"

"I found it." She popped up with her purse. "Bye, everybody! It was so great meeting you all!" she called out.

Theo groaned. *Damn, I was so close.*

The mob converged, kissing and hugging, drawing it out into the longest goodbye *ever*. Even his baby cousin begged her to come to the *quince* on Saturday, which was fine with him because that was another day guaranteed together. He was starting to worry that she'd get rid of him after the class and that was *no bueno*. Every part of his long-term plans involved him and Reina. *That's it.*

It took a lifetime, but eventually he led Reina toward a path on the side of the house, grabbing her hand and soaking in the night. It was a perfect spring evening. No clouds and thousands of stars, walking with his *jeva*.

They squeezed between the tightly packed stucco homes and walked further away from the house, not toward the street but away.

"Wait, why aren't we walking back to my car?" Reina looked around her. "Is it parked over here?" She stopped. "You don't have another motorcycle stashed back here, do you?"

"Is that excitement I hear in your voice? About riding again?" He laughed.

"A little? The best part was when I sat behind you and touched you as much as I wanted. Maybe I'll be able to ride one again someday."

"Yeah." He squeezed her hand and walked through a canopy of bougainvillea trees. "Go back to talking about the touching part. About the touching *me* part."

She looked up at him, a wide grin spreading across her face. "I'd be happy to tell you what I was feeling *and* what I was thinking."

Theo's cock surged. His girl liked to talk, and it always made him hard, especially when she shared how she felt. "Make the words."

"Well, I was scared to death at first but then I pressed my cheek against your back, and even through your jacket, I could smell you."

"Smell me? Is that good?" He swore by his cologne, but he was a physical guy.

"Amazing." She giggled. "You have the best smell. It reminds me of late nights, deep kisses, and me riding your face for hours."

Theo threw his head back and laughed harder than he had in years. He slung an arm over her shoulders and kissed her through her giggles. "Tell me more."

"After I relaxed and saw you weren't going to drive like a maniac…"

"You calling me crazy?"

"Definitely." She grabbed the hand hanging over her shoulder. "I realized that I could touch you as much as I wanted."

"I remember." He groaned, fucking out of his mind when her little hand snuck under his shirt and brushed his abs. "Tell me what you were thinking when you did it."

"Well," she pressed her hands to her cheeks, "I was thinking about touching you and how beautiful you looked with your shirt off in the gym."

"No one has ever thought that I'm beautiful except for you."

"What? Impossible. I have the best taste." She smiled. "I thought there couldn't be anything better than touching you," she peeked up at him, "until I realized I could do it with my tongue. I wanted to taste you so badly, I couldn't think. I was going to jump you but then you turned on the motorcycle and I freaked out."

His body went rigid. Touch… mouth… His brain shut down. He scooped her up in his arms.

"*Theo.*"

"You walk too slow." In two seconds flat, he ran through a large gate that separated his backyard from his mother's.

"You live behind your family?" She peered over his shoulder. "You *are* a mama's boy, aren't you?" She gasped. "What a cute swing."

The backyard had been a pet project. He'd spent years building a deck, a treehouse with a swing, everything his future family might want. He balanced her in one arm and reached in his pocket for his keys.

"That's the biggest doghouse I've ever seen."

"It belongs to Shadow." He managed to fit the key in the door. "He's already outgrown it."

"What kind of dog is he?"

"An English Mastiff. He's still a puppy, so he's only about one-forty. He's got another forty to go."

"Pounds? I didn't even know dogs came that big." She looked around. "Where is he?"

"There's a doggy door between the two properties. He has the run of both houses. My mom probably has him locked up with the little kids. They like to lie all over him like a rug."

"Well, I think your place is adorable."

"I think you mean manly and tough. Like me." He pried open the door and almost fell in with Reina in his arms.

"That's what I meant. Super manly and so tough. I especially noticed when you gave advice to your baby cousin." She kissed the side of his neck. "I love seeing that side of you. Makes you even sexier."

Even sexier? His knees buckled as he claimed her mouth, kicking the door shut before heading to the bedroom.

"You're the best kisser."

Theo threw her on his unmade bed. "I'm going down on you again. Are you going to pull out your manual?"

"Not if I'm on top." She grinned, her cheeks blushing prettily.

"If that's what it takes for you to finish. Hell yeah. But..." He backed up and opened his dresser drawer. "I have a surprise for you. But only if I get to see you."

"You know I'm shy about that."

Don't push, pendejo. He watched as she sucked on her lip, unable to meet his eye. "How about we start slow, but the minute you want to change things up, you let me know. And yes, you still get your surprise, no matter how we do it."

She sat up on her elbows. "I like surprises."

He rummaged around in his drawer. "Close your eyes. Don't open until you feel me by you." He pointed at her and went to his bathroom. "Don't move."

"Why are you always saying that to me?" she grumbled, looking absolutely adorable, eventually flopping back on the bed and shutting her lids.

"Feel free to start stripping." Theo shut the door and opened his mouth, removing his tongue ring. It came off with a final tug, and he placed it in a cleaning solution. *Time for Reina's surprise.* Popping the lid, he studied the pink silicone device, taking a few minutes to figure out how it worked. The little rocket vibrated softly. *Perfect.* He attached it to his tongue, the bulk a little uncomfortable.

"I have to admit I'm getting a little nervous." Reina gripped the sheets.

Theo kneeled on the bed, spreading Reina's pretty legs. He peppered a few kisses on her knee to settle her. Her scarf was already gone, and her fitted red dress with black tights begged to be removed. But he'd follow the rules. So far, there was no agreement about skin. So he'd have to be persuasive.

"Theo?"

"Shh." He wanted to go straight for the goods, but he'd been *dying* to feast on her breasts. So he brushed them with his cheek, feeling her nipples pebble through the fitted material. Unable to resist, he opened his mouth wide and sucked on her pert areolas.

"That feels so good. But what's that bumpy thing?"

Instead of answering, he pressed on a button at the bottom of the vibrating tongue ring and turned it on.

"What's that noise?" She grabbed his hair and tried to pull him back, but he stayed connected to her plump breasts. "That sounds like my vibrator."

He feasted on her other breast, soaking in her gasped cry.

"*Omigod.*" Her eyes popped open and she grabbed his chin. "Open up." He did and she whispered, "You have a vibrating tongue ring? Jesus, Mary and Joseph, I can't take this."

"Take of your shirt." Which sounded more like *thake op yu shirp*, but he thought she got the message, her wide eyes studying his mouth.

"I can do that." She unbuttoned her dress down to her waist. "I want you to see them."

He was floored. Why the change of heart? He'd had to beg her the other night.

"I'm self-conscious about VJs, but I love my breasts. I can't wait to feel that vibrating thingy on them." She slipped out of the sleeves and reached for her bra.

He loved this confident Reina. He'd been dreaming about this day for months, and he couldn't wait for her to unwrap that package.

"Theo?"

He couldn't look away from her black lace bra, and her plump breasts peeking over the top.

"Are they as beautiful as you imagined?" Her wicked grin went straight to his strained cock. She pulled down her bra cups, exposing luscious mounds that bounced into her palms, filling them with soft warm flesh.

He grunted, unable to speak. Her coral nipples were perfect, puckered, and begging for his mouth. He pushed away her hands and took his time nuzzling under her breasts, rubbing the nipple with his nose, surrounding and sliding around them. He breathed in deep, surrounding himself with her essence. When he couldn't stand it another second, he took her areola in his mouth and groaned as he tasted her, playing the toy over her nipple.

Her back arched up. "Best thing I ever felt. My nipples are so sensitive." She moaned.

He tightened her bra, trapping it under her plump pillows so they were pushed up and ready for his eager mouth. He lavished them with attention, using the toy mercilessly until she was begging him for relief.

"I need more."

He pulled back and looked between her thighs, frustrated the vibrating tongue ring stopped him from describing her beauty. Her eyes were at half mast, her lips wet from his kisses, her gorgeous breasts on display. She was the most gorgeous thing he'd ever seen.

He pushed his face between her legs.

She jumped. "S-sorry, I got a little excited. That wasn't as strong as I thought it would be." She moaned when he went back in, licking her through her tights and panties.

If she wants me, she needs to say it.

"Harder, Theo!"

But he kept a soft pace, breathing in her essence, the heated musk surrounding him, making his throbbing cock smash against his jeans.

She grabbed his hair. "Take off my tights."

He cocked a brow and waited.

"You stubborn man, you want the panties off too, right? Take them off." She grabbed her breasts and pinched her nipples. *Hell yes.* Best sight ever.

He slipped his hands under her dress and yanked her tights and panties off her legs.

"Yes! So sexy. I love those tights and I don't even care."

He got an up close view of her glistening sex. God, she was beautiful. Her plump pink folds begging for his mouth. He couldn't wait, didn't bother with torturing her. He needed her wet sex in his mouth. Now.

He went down fast, careful of his placement, moving around her clit until she found her rhythm.

"God, yes. Like that, baby. I'm going to come so fast!" She

arched her back. "I'm coming. For you. *Just for you,*" she whispered.

Her silky release coated his face, her juices flooding him. He licked up every drop, lapping and sucking until she pulled at his hair. He growled in response, but she begged him so sweetly.

"Theo, stop. *Please.* I'm too sensitive." She slumped back when he stopped.

Theo felt like a sexual timebomb, his dick ready to explode. He palmed himself and Reina's eyes went wide. She wore the most perfect, blissed-out smile he'd ever seen. It made him groan.

"Your turn."

He turned off the vibrator. He wanted to tell her so much, but he couldn't think properly. Perfect breasts, glistening lips, he'd never seen anything that turned him on more. He fumbled with his zipper.

"I have an idea. Come here, baby. Let me do that for you."

He leaned into her, letting her unbuckle his pants. Finally he sprang free, an infinitesimal amount of pressure, relieved. *"Guh,"* was the only thing he could managed to say.

"Let me take care of you." She pulled his jeans down under his dick. "You're so beautiful." She looked up at him in awe. "You're pierced here, too." She ran her finger down his torso, where it met his shaft. Two silver barbells glistened in the light. "I'm obsessed with it already."

He moaned, made weak by her words. He thrust forward, and she ran her hand up his length. He clasped his palm over hers, squeezing tight. He didn't have the stamina for exploration. He needed release.

"Wait. Not yet." She sat up on her knees. "I need some lube. Do you have any?"

No. There was no time!

"I can feel you yelling at me with your eyes." She giggled. "I'll make do." She dipped her fingers into her glistening sex, moaning as she coated her fingers and used her release to glaze his cock. *Dios mio!* He could feel his semen climbing up his cock. The sight of her floored him.

"Don't come yet. It's going to be so good, baby." She leaned over him. "Let me position myself. I've been dreaming about giving you a boob job from the first time you stared at my breasts."

Boob what? He pinched the end of his cock, but it might be too late.

"Now, come between my breasts." She placed her chest by his straining cock, pushing forward as her full mounds surrounded him in the softest pillows he'd ever felt. "Let go, I've got you." She squeezed her breasts together with her arms, creating the softest friction.

One pump. Not gonna make it long. Two pumps. He fisted the sheet. Three pumps and pleasure raced up his spine. *Yes!* As his release barreled through him, Reina clamped her mouth around his mushroom head, and swallowed him deep.

He bellowed to the ceiling, on overload from the combination of her taste in his tongue, her soft breasts, and now her mouth around his cock. He came with her name on his lips, until he collapsed on the bed, wrapping her up in his arms.

He held tight and planned to tell her how much she meant to him once he got the tongue ring out. His little beauty surprised him every day, making each one better than the last. And for once, in a very long time, he felt complete.

Chapter 21

DOING YOUR A, B, CS

THURSDAY

REN WOKE WITH a start, a soft snuffling sound rousing her from sleep. Blurry from beautiful VJs, Ren blinked open heavy lids and came face-to-face with a dark, soul-filled gaze. Ren yipped and jumped back, scrambling away from the specter looming over her. A writhing mass who seemed to…pant, a lot.

A giant tan dog, the biggest she'd ever seen, thumped his thick tail on the carpet, its pink tongue dangling out of its drooly mouth.

"Good morning, beautiful." Ren sat up and looked around, petting the drooly but super-sweet doggie.

There was enough light coming in from the living room to illuminate Theo's bedroom. It looked like a bomb had gone off. Clothes were strewn on the floor, shoes everywhere…and piles of books. Super geeky math stuff that made her toes curl. She also spotted a video game console and a ton of old games.

Theo's a slob.

Luckily, it looked more messy than dirty, which she could live with. It meant his mama didn't clean his house for him.

The dog bumped her hand. Maybe he was hungry. Or saying

good morning? She didn't speak dog, had never had one growing up. "How did you get over here?" Then she remembered the doggy door that took up half the front entrance. "It's nice to meet you." She peeked under his belly. "Yup, definitely a boy. What did Theo say your name was? Shadow?" She kissed his head, and he swiped a pink tongue along her cheek.

Eww.

Ren stood and carefully tiptoed around the room, looking for her clothes. Everything was off. She didn't usually sleep in the nude—ever. She always at least had her panties on. Apparently, there were no rules when she was around Teófilo. She giggled, considering whether she liked that name better than Theo. Teo sounded nice, too.

The object of her musings was sprawled out on the bed, face first and naked as a jaybird. The white sheet sat below his magnificent ass. It might be the best thing she'd ever seen. The image burned into her brain, and she fought the urge to lean down and take a bite out of his perfect ass.

She glanced at the side clock and almost fell over. Six in the morning! Shit! She hadn't planned on spending the night, but two orgasms had taken it out of her. Today, of all days, she couldn't be late. She shivered even as she raced around throwing on her dress.

How could I forget?

The anniversary of Nicholas' accident. His mother would expect her there, and she didn't want to keep her waiting. She'd gone through so much after losing her son. He was her whole world, her only child, and she still hadn't completely accepted the permanence of his situation.

Ren tugged on her boots, tempted beyond measure to slip back under the sheets with Theo, obviously the deepest sleeper she'd ever met. She and Shadow looked at him. Ren patted the dog's head and whispered, "I'm sorry. I'd feed you if I could, but I don't know where your daddy keeps the food. Or how much to give you."

Unwilling to mar the perfect picture of Theo fast asleep, she tiptoed around to find her purse and keys. Blowing a kiss to Theo, she grabbed her stuff and walked into the living room. It was a little less messy than the bedroom. The small bungalow had built-in bookshelves and hardwood floors. A bachelor pad that definitely felt like Theo.

She looked through the window at the swing. Unbelievable. He was the biggest, scariest guy she'd ever met, but deep down he was a total softie. She loved that about him—along with his intense glare, sexy frown, and talented tongue.

Her knees went weak when she thought about the two incredible orgasms he'd rung out of her. And when she'd returned the favor, taking him deep between her breasts, to make him as crazed as she had been… mind blowing. To keep herself from jumping his bones, she walked over to a wooden bench that ran the length of the back wall. It was littered with framed photos, and she picked one up, hoping to see pictures of Theo as a kid.

The first was of Alexei, Theo, and a fresh-faced girl with enormous dark eyes and black hair. They all looked to be pre-teens, and Theo had thick glasses and…he was chubby! Oh my gosh, he was the cutest thing she'd ever seen. The next was Theo and the same girl, but even younger. She gazed at the camera, he at her. There were more of Alexei and Theo, some of his family, but almost every picture was of Rosie.

She returned to the photo of the two of them, and she studied the look on his face. It wasn't one she recognized. Pure love blazed from him, engulfing his young face, making him look aglow with happiness. Some might explain it away as puppy love, but whatever it was, he was consumed with it.

It felt so different from the way he looked at her. Every glance now contained intensity tinged with a bit of sadness. The loss of Rosie had devastated Theo, and it became really clear that he remained intensely connected to her memory.

Not that I'm one to talk.

Stepping back with a last pat to Shadow, who'd been leaning against her legs the entire time, she glanced around to make sure she hadn't forgotten anything. Until she realized the photos weren't only on the side table. They were everywhere. *Rosie* was everywhere. Even a hand painted portrait hung over the fireplace. Unable to resist, she tiptoed back to Theo. Even more photos littered the bedroom, plus stacks of condolence cards and letters. It made her stomach twist in knots.

On one hand, she absolutely understood and adored Theo's devotion. He must miss Rosie so much. But it also left her feeling queasy. His home was basically a shrine to his ex-girlfriend, which was none of her business, but it didn't look like he was a man ready to move on from his loss.

We're two sides of the same coin.

Her phone beeped, reminding her she had to go. She hugged Shadow and slipped out of the bungalow, wondering what this meant for their future—one haunted by the memories of their loss.

Chapter 22

DINING DOWNTOWN

*P*ING.

Ren ignored her phone and rushed through the skilled nursing facility. This was about the tenth time it had gone off, and it didn't take a rocket scientist to figure out it was Theo. She'd sent him a quick text after she'd gotten home, not wanting him to think she'd blown him off. But she'd been too busy getting ready and racing her late butt over here to call him back.

If she were honest, a not-so-tiny part of her had been freaked out by the Rosie shrine. The night before, sharing their stories about loss had connected her to Theo. He'd showed her how amazingly caring he could be, but if he was still tethered to his ex, emotionally, it would never work between them. It only reminded her of her own guilt about cutting ties. Rounding a corner, she came face-to-face with Señora Gonzalez.

"*Mija*, you're late!" Nicholas' mom reached out, but let her hand drop before she touched Ren's light-pink wig. "What is this?"

It was her newest beauty, and she thought the long length and cut would lift her spirits. Today was the worst day of the year for her. "Do you like it? I just got it." Ren engulfed the plump woman in a hug.

"I've never seen you look like this. What would Nicholas think? He's only ever known you before your...problems."

"Alopecia."

"What? Yes, yes." She straightened her jacket. "What if he woke up? And saw you like this." She clasped the door handle, her face getting red. "Please, I don't want anything to be different. It must remain the same. You know that. He wouldn't even recognize you."

Was that true? Ren took a step back, rocked by Señora Gonzalez's words. Nicholas had been beautiful and full of life, and he'd loved her hair. He'd also been reckless and impulsive, but never shallow. Either way, she would have known in two seconds flat what he thought. Good or bad, he never held back. And for whatever reason, that made her smile. It was also unfair to judge him by his eighteen-year-old self. Years had passed, who knew the man he would have become.

"Please, *mija*. He loved your dark hair. This would be too much for him. You understand?" When Ren didn't immediately answer, she said, "Promise me!" Her round face grew flushed.

Ren opened her mouth to respond, knowing this woman had experienced immeasurable grief. There was no need to argue. So she bit her tongue, like she always did. "I'll remember next time."

No, I won't, she whispered to herself. Even if she didn't have the courage to say it out loud, she would never change who she'd fought so hard to become. *But* why *can't I say it out loud?* Because the guilt weighed too heavily.

"Should we go in?" Ren sat down next to Nicholas and smiled when she saw the familiar shock of dark hair standing on end. He always had the unruliest mop. Ren focused on that instead of the tubes and machines surrounding him.

"We're here, *mijo. Tu amá* and your beautiful fiancée, Adrenilda. We came to visit you." Señora Gonzalez fussed around him, straightening the pillow and smoothing down the blanket.

Ren stiffened, once again unable to voice her truth. She wasn't his fiancée, but Señora Gonzalez had fixated on the dream. The one where the two of them would marry after college. But their differences became glaringly clear after they'd graduated. Ren had broken up with him, realizing they were first loves that were never meant to last into adulthood. But Señora Gonzalez was as stuck as Nicholas, frozen in time from years ago when the tragic accident had occurred.

Ren's *tía* warned her every time they spoke that she wasn't doing the woman any favors. She'd cautioned she was only making it harder in the long run, but what did the little white lie cost her? She wanted to ease Senora Gonzalez's pain, not contribute to it. Ren knew in her heart of hearts that Nicholas would never come out of the coma. Never. But his mother still held out hope, and she wanted life to remain static for when he emerged.

Ren stayed back, allowing his mother her time with him, all the while thinking about Theo and his connection to Rosie. He had only hinted at the trauma, but after seeing the look on his face in those pictures, she wondered if he was ready to move on. Could either of them truly give themselves to someone new? Her present was as intertwined with Nicholas as her past. And Theo, maybe even more so.

Ping.

Señora Gonzalez spun around and killed her with a look. She didn't like interruptions during their visits.

"Sorry." Ren gripped the strap of her bag, resisting the urge to check her messages. Theo had probably left her a few hundred more. From the moment they'd met at speed dating, he'd liked to check in throughout the day. It hadn't bothered her before now, but today, with the anniversary of the accident, she wanted to focus on Nicholas without any distractions.

Coward, she whispered to herself. *You're running away*. Falling into old patterns of avoid, avoid, avoid.

Which doubled her guilt.

"Don't leave him alone. Tell him I'll be right back." Señora Gonzalez stood, wiping away a few tears. "I need to talk to the nurse. I'll be back, *mijo*."

Ren watched her leave, wondering about Nicholas' mother's erratic behavior. It seemed over the top, even for her.

Taking a deep breath, now that she had a little space, Ren took the opportunity to sit next to Nicholas. "Long time no see." She smiled and brushed back his midnight locks. It'd only been a few days since her last visit. His mother had no idea she dropped in a few times a month, visiting as late as possible so they could have a little alone time.

Ren missed talking to him the most. "Remember that guy I told you about? The one who asked for my number? Well, we finally spoke to each other a few days ago, and I've seen him every night since. I think you'd like him. You two would get into a lot of trouble together."

It had taken a few years to accept Nicholas for who he was, not who he was supposed to be. Because of it, she was so grateful she could still touch him and talk to him. For too long, she wallowed in the anger of the loss, watching him slowly fade away.

But today, she felt more selfish than usual. Today, she missed her bestie. And ultimately, even though Señora Gonzalez wouldn't acknowledge it, they'd been better friends than lovers. Nicholas had known it was true, but he'd had a harder time accepting it. The last time they'd spoken, it had been a huge blow out.

I'd do anything to change that night.

"I love you and miss you every day." She kissed his forehead and wiped the tears from under her eyes.

Señora Gonzalez charged in, bustling and energetic as ever.

"Did you have a nice talk? One day, when he wakes up, he'll see that we've been here for him. He'll be so proud of his beautiful fiancée."

"Are you okay, Señora?" Ren walked over to her and clasped her hands.

"I'm fine." But the stalwart woman wouldn't meet her eyes. "I want to make sure he's happy. And that he always knows I'm here for him."

"He does. He loves you so much." Ren frowned, worried the stress was too much.

"It's this facility. They're saying things I don't agree with." She squeezed Ren's hands. "But I know I have you. You'll take care of him. You'll always help."

"Of course." She wrapped the trembling woman in her arms. "Always, I promise."

"Good, good. He has you." Señora patted her hand and squared her shoulders. "One day he'll be awake and see how hard we fought for him. How much we believed he would get better." She made the sign of the cross and sat back next to Nicholas. "You'll have the most beautiful wedding."

Ren took a deep breath, studying the deep lines of the older woman's face. These last years had aged her, hope not enough to sustain her through the devastation of her loss. How could Ren correct her now after so many years? Who was it hurting to let her believe she and Nicholas were engaged?

It's killing you, she whispered to herself.

Nicholas would never come out of his coma. His body had deteriorated and he'd had no brain activity from the beginning. But just as Ren understood he wouldn't awaken; Señora Gonzalez believed he would. She glanced down at him and his grieving mother. "I'll always be here for you both."

Señora Gonzalez nodded and then got back to plumping his pillow and adjusting the angle of the bed.

"I have to get back to work." Ren paused at the door, feeling the weight of her secret. Soon, she'd have to tell her the truth because experiencing joy and fun and orgasms with Theo taught her she deserved a full life. "It was good seeing you."

"You too, *mija.* And remember, natural is always better." She dismissed Ren with a wave over her shoulder.

Ren sighed but nodded, quickly making her way toward her car to go to work.

Chapter 23

SIPPING FROM THE HONEY POT

REN SAT IN her car after work, still parked in the underground parking structure, her forehead resting against the steering wheel. *I've messed everything up.* Her brain whirled, and she knew her inaction might have ruined her fledgling relationship. She hadn't returned Theo's calls. Her morning surprise and then Señora Gonzalez's over-the-top encounter had set her on edge.

Ren had retreated. Fallen back on old habits where she powered through her difficulties… alone. But now that the bustle of the hospital was behind her, she had no distractions to keep her from Theo.

She turned on her phone.

Ping, ping, ping, pingpingping…

Swiping down, she saw she had close to twenty missed texts. Plus a few voicemail messages. Quickly skimming, she read:

Didn't like waking up without you.

Got your text. Checking in.

What time we hooking up tonight?

Talk to me, Reina.

If I fucked this up, let me know.

TALK TO ME.

Message received.

Shit. He was pissed, and he had every right to be. But she'd needed space, a little time to go over their relationship. Or lack thereof. Not that she'd decided everything over the day except one thing.

We need to talk.

She called Theo, no answer. "If you get this, I can explain everything. Call me. I'm so sorry." She texted a few times repeating the apology, but as she drove down the street with no return call, she knew things were bad.

Driving over to his place wasn't an option because she had to get home to Brynn. Glancing at her car console, she saw it was close to eight o'clock. The Ladies would be leaving soon, so she gave Brynn a call to say she was on the way.

Brynn picked up on the first ring, breathless and giggling. "Ren? Guess what? Alexei finished up early and he's home." Her voice sounded muffled, and Ren thought she heard a breathy moan.

"That's great news."

"Yeah. You're free tonight. You can see Theo, and you don't have to babysit me."

"I didn't do a very good job. I hardly saw you."

"Are you kidding me? You were a lifesaver. Thank you so much."

"I owe you, Ren." A deep voice, obviously Alexei, chimed in.

"You guys don't owe me anything." Tears sprang to her eyes. She was happy for her friend but a little confused about her own relationship. "Since your sexy Alexei is there, I think I'll head home tonight. Give you guys some privacy."

"Okay. Alexei, *stop*." More giggling. "Are you sure, Ren? You don't have to drive all the way home tonight. You can come here if it's closer."

"No, actually I live in Eagle Rock, so it'll take me less time to get to my house." *This is all my fault.* Truly. Ren was incapable of managing any of her relationships, but since she had Brynn and Theo's best friend on the phone… "Um, hey, can I ask you something really quick?"

"I don't know. Can you?" Brynn giggled.

She is such a teacher. "*May* I ask you something?"

"Sure. Let me… Okay, just me or both of us?"

"Both, please."

After a few muffled seconds, Alexei said, "You're on speaker."

"Okay." Ren cleared her throat, completely in over her head. How to broach the topic of her total lack of experience with men, relationships, and moody MMA fighters? "I wanted to ask for some advice about Theo."

"Ask," Alexei said, true to form as a man of few words.

"We're here for whatever you need," Brynn chimed in.

"What's the best way to deal with Theo when he gets mad?"

"Same way you deal with him every other time you see him," Alexei said.

"What do you mean?" Ren searched one handed for her keys, rummaging around her bag.

"He's always mad," Alexei said. "He generally hates people, so it happens a lot."

"That's not true." Ren felt protective of Theo in that moment. She'd seen him with his family, with some of the other MMA fighters. He didn't hate *everybody.*

"It's not?" Alexei laughed. "Now that I think about it, he doesn't hate you."

"I know he's kind of grumpy, but he's never been angry with me. Until today. I kind of messed up, and I think he might be done with me." She sniffled, furious that she was having such a strong reaction. They hadn't known each other long enough for this, but the guilt was killing her.

"I'm sorry, sweets. Please don't cry," Brynn intoned. "What did he say to you?"

"He didn't." She cleared her throat. "He's ignoring my calls."

Dead silence.

With each beat of her wounded heart, the certainty grew. She'd done irreparable harm. "I messed up, right?" Her voice hitched. "I had a difficult day, and I needed time to process. I ignored his calls."

Alexi finally answered, "He doesn't do well with that. Because of a bunch of reasons, he gets crazed. If it gets too bad, he disconnects."

"That's what I was worried about." Rosie's death had changed him, made him assume the worst, and Ren had contributed to his pain. She hated that she'd done that. Even if he never saw her again, it would kill her if she'd done damage to his fragile heart. She thought of how he held her when he'd thought her hair loss meant she was ill. "I really messed up."

"Ren, I didn't know it was a bad day. Come over, and we can talk in person," Brynn said.

"No, you guys need some alone time. And I need to fix this." She pulled up to her apartment. "Any suggestions on how I can reach him? Or make this better?"

"Most of the time he rides up in the mountains when he's upset. Sometimes he takes off for days."

"O-on his motorcycle?" Her hands shook as she slammed her car door shut. Her own devastating fears crashed to the surface. If anything happened it would be her fault... all over again.

Please God, let him be okay.

"Yeah. I'll try to reach him and tell him you're looking for him."

"Thanks. I have to go. Bye." She hung up quickly, lost in her thoughts. History might be repeating itself and there was nothing she could do to prevent it.

Chapter 24

GOING SOUTH WITH THE MOUTH

THEO BRACED FOR the blow, sensing he hadn't reacted fast enough. The right hook smashed him right under his eye, throwing him off balance.

His nose popped, and then felt like it caught on fire. Trying to shake off the pain, he rubbed his eyeballs that felt like they'd been scooped out. He knew what that meant. Double black eyes.

Focus, *pendejo*.

If you don't stop thinking about Reina, you're going to fall on your ass in front of everyone. You. Do. Not. Lose. The fury at not hearing from her blasted him into action, and he pummeled the boxer, going in much harder than he needed to. Blow after blow, even when he was on the ground—

"Hey, hey, hey!" Tommy, the owner of the gym, slammed into him and wrestled him to the ground. "Enough, man. *Jesus.* What the hell is wrong with you?"

"Let me up!" Theo's chest heaved as he gulped in air, still in survival mode.

"Hell, no." Tommy had him in a chokehold and on the ground, progressively adding pressure. "You need to calm the fuck down. How many times do I have to tell you this shit?"

The red haze subsided, eventually, and Theo glanced over at the injured fighter. They'd sparred more than once, but Theo wasn't in the right headspace for a fair fight. *Shit.* His opponent hadn't deserved the beat down. "I'm good! Get off me. I swear."

"That's it! I gave you too many fucking chances. You're done. Banned. Stay the fuck out of my gym. Don't come back!" The furious ginger stormed off, slamming his office door.

Damn. Tommy was the nicest until you sparked his temper. It hadn't been the first time he'd been pissed at Theo, but he'd never banned him before.

Blue sauntered over, leaning in on the ropes as he called off the other fighters that were ready to spring in to fight.

Theo popped up and walked over to the *veterano,* the OG fighter who deserved better.

"Tommy just let you up. I *will* beat your ass if you start throwing blows again." Blue pointed at Theo, but didn't stop him from approaching the fighter.

"Try it." Theo scoffed, his eyes watering so much he could hardly see the guy swaying in front of him. "Good job, man. You stayed on your feet." Theo clapped him on the back. "And you gave me two shiners."

"I'm getting too old for this shit, *ese.*" The fighter worked his jaw and grinned.

"Catch you next time." Theo slammed him again on the back for good measure and made his way out to the locker rooms. Passing Alexei's office made the haze creep back in. Memories of Reina riding his face were like strobe lights through his mind. The anger took over, but so did his love sick cock.

Calm the fuck down, loser. She doesn't want you, he directed at his granite dick.

It didn't listen.

"What the hell's up with you? I thought you were all blissed out with your girl. What the hell happened in there?" Blue followed him into the lockers.

Theo grabbed a towel and wrapped it around his waist, not wanting to broadcast his tent pole. "I lost it for a minute. But I'm good now."

"You're not if Tommy can't trust you in there. You're a trainer. They aren't your personal punching bags. You're lucky you were in the ring with an experienced fighter. You would have done permanent damage to one of the trainees."

Theo banged open his locker and pulled out jeans and a long-sleeved tee.

"Tell me what's going on. Maybe I can help." Blue leaned against the lockers as Theo stripped down.

"I don't know where she is!" He threw the clothes down and headed for the shower.

"Who?" Blue frowned, his dark brows slashing over storm-gray eyes. "Ren?"

"Yeah, she won't answer my calls. We were together last night."

"Did you fight?" Blue shook his head. "Or say something stupid?"

"No." He slapped the tile and quickly washed down. "It was amazing. At least, I thought it was amazing. She obviously didn't."

"But what if she's hurt? Maybe we need to call Sebastian. He's a cop." Blue reached in his pocket and took out his phone.

"No." Theo blew out a deep breath. "I checked with the hospital. She went to work but didn't answer my calls." He shut off the faucet and dried off. When he grabbed his jeans, a rock fell out of his pocket.

"What's that?"

"Holy shit. It's a crystal. Reina uses them for healing or protection." He gripped it like a lifeline, a tiny kernel of hope unfurling in his chest. She wouldn't have given it to him if she didn't care. Would she? "It looks different from the one she had me hold at the hospital. This one is black. She must have slipped it in my pocket."

"That's cool. Let me see."

"No! It's mine."

"Jesus Christ." Blue laughed. "Didn't you ever learn to share?"

He clutched the crystal to his chest, not wanting Blue to get his bad juju all over it.

"I don't know what to tell you except, keep trying. Call her. Have you checked your phone? You were sparring for hours."

"I shut it off so I'd stop looking. It was driving me nuts. That's why I needed to burn some energy in the ring."

"You took it too far. You're not fighting for *la mafia* anymore. This isn't life or death situations. Most of our customers are newbs. You know that. Tommy hasn't built up his reputation for the elites. Yet." Blue shook his head, clearly disappointed. It was a change for the mellow loner. Before the last few days, he usually never bothered to get involved in shit like this. That was why they got along.

He'd patch things up with Tommy and Blue another time. Right now, all he could think about was Reina. When had it all gone wrong?

Last night had been a dream. His family had loved her. *Tío* Hugo was going to kill him if he didn't come home with her, but he wouldn't be surprised. The whole family had made it pretty clear she was too good for him.

"Turn on your damn phone, man. What have you got to lose?"

Theo reached into his locker, afraid to look. After a few swipes, his phone went silent. "You see—"

Hum, crackle, hum crackle, humcracklehum.

"Does your phone sound like a lightsaber?" Blue asked.

"Yes. Shut up, it's my notifications." His phone blew up with texts and messages, and his entire body eased the tiniest bit. It was Reina, but she'd offered no explanation. There were a few missed calls, a text with her address, and an invite to come over.

"Well?" Blue crowded in over his shoulder. "What did she say?"

"That's private."

"You better tell me. You almost killed somebody. You obviously need help. And I am a dating professional." He tapped his chest and smiled.

"Is that what they call fuckboys these days?"

"You trying to pick a fight with me, too? I'm your last friend around here."

"You're right. Sorry." The word felt thick on his tongue, but his friend had tried to help "There was no explanation, just a promise to explain everything if I come over."

"There you go. That's sounds pretty straight-forward to me."

"But she ignored me *all day*. After we spent the night together. I haven't heard from her in twelve hours."

"How long have you been dating this girl?"

"I met her six months ago at the volleyball game." Theo rammed his phone in his back pocket.

"I call bullshit. You didn't even talk to her." Blue put his hands on his hips. "When was the first time you spoke to her in person? It doesn't even have to be a date."

"A few days ago." Theo winced, knowing it sounded crazy. But they had a connection, a deep one, and he didn't deserve to be ignored. "Don't fucking say it." He pointed at Blue.

"You're insane." He slapped Theo on the back, and they walked out of the gym. "And if you push her too far, you're going to mess it up."

"That's coming from a guy who's never gone on a second date?" Theo pushed him as they walked out of the gym. "I don't take advice from whores."

"Fuck off." Blue remained unbothered. Probably because he knew it was true.

"When you know, you know. I can't be expected to make someone like you understand."

"You'd be surprised." The perpetually even-tempered fighter's face hardened, and then he shrugged it off. "So, what? You saying you know she's the one after a few days?"

"I knew six months ago." Theo pushed open the glass doors with a hard shove and walked back to his bike. He'd picked it up earlier in the day from the charm school.

"Then go. She asked you over. Listen to her. Get out of your own head and understand it isn't only about you." Blue grabbed his helmet and straddled the bike next to Theo's. "And don't fuck it up with your temper. Chill the fuck out. Like me." He smiled and revved the engine.

"Thanks, *acere*."

Chapter 25

HUM JOB

THEO PULLED UP to the long driveway, barely registering Ren's three-story, Spanish-style apartment building. She'd told him she was on the first floor, apartment A4. He shut off his bike. He couldn't bring himself to knock on Reina's door. His emotions were a toxic mix of anger and worry.

Blue's words floated away. They held no weight. Because he couldn't understand her. Why ghost him? It had taken months to get them to the point of connecting. He never thought they'd take this many steps back. He'd been so convinced something had happened to her, he'd called the hospital and waited until she answered. When she'd said hello, sounding as happy as ever, he couldn't speak, couldn't believe she'd ignored him.

He took off his helmet and looked up at the cloudless sky. Millions of stars dotted the velvet night. Out of habit, he looked for the star that was the furthest away, the smallest and hardest to detect. The one that should receive acknowledgment because it fought the hardest to be seen.

The one just like me.

He thought Reina *saw* him, but maybe Blue was right, and it was too much to expect in a few days.

Right now, despite the brew of sentiments sitting in his stomach, he needed to hear her voice again to know she was all right. It was half past midnight. Imagining her curled up and rumpled in bed got him hard again.

He gripped his phone, ready to dial her when he saw the email notification. The same message that had been sitting unopened, all day. The email he'd received this morning from USC, the one that would tell him what his life would be like for the next four years. He'd wanted to open it with Reina, and when she'd ignored him, he couldn't bring himself to read it alone.

Ignoring the stupid email, he stabbed his phone and held his breath.

"Hello?" She cleared her throat, and repeated, "Hello? Theo? Is that you?"

"I'm here."

"I'm glad you called." She sighed.

Deep, dark silence filled the space between words.

"Were you riding in the hills? On your bike?"

How had she known that had been his first choice of escape? Before he could take off, he'd remembered her terror about him riding. Even when he hadn't heard from her in hours, he still opted out of utilizing his sure-fire release mechanism. That was why he'd headed toward Tommy's and taken it out on a fighter.

He had to admit, a tiny part of him hadn't wanted to be too far away in case she called him back. *Pathetic.* "No."

"Oh, thank God," she whispered. "I'm so glad you're okay."

"I'm fine." It had been *seconds,* and she still hadn't explained.

"Were you smashing your beautiful brain?" She used *Tío's* description of his mafia fights.

"I smash *them.* They don't smash me." He winced when lifting his eyebrows was a reminder of his two black eyes. "Usually."

"Come over, please. I have a lot to tell you, and I want to do it in person. Wait, what time is it?" She rustled around again. "Shoot.

It's almost one a.m. I guess it's too late for you to drive all the way over here."

"I'm too pissed to come in. The only reason I called was to make sure you were still alive." The knot in his chest still hadn't eased.

"Theo. Didn't you call me at work already to find that out?"

Shit. Busted.

"I knew it was you." He heard a click as if she was turning on a bedside light. "Even before I look at my phone, I always know when it's you."

"How?"

"I don't know. I just do." Her sleepy voice hitched. "I'm messing this up, but I'd hoped to apologize in person. This has been a hard day, but I'm sorry I didn't text you and explain about what was going on."

"Why didn't you?" The words burst out from the deepest part of his chest. "You know that fucks with my head."

"You're right. This is all my fault. But even if you never want to speak to me again, I hope you'll let me apologize. I don't like hurting people. Especially people who are important to me."

I'm important?

"I wish it wasn't too late for me to see you."

Damn, he felt his cold heart melting, but he wasn't anywhere near letting this go. Still, he found himself saying, "You said it was too late. I didn't."

"Then you'll come?" The springs on her bed squeaked. "I know! I'll come to you. It's the least I can—"

"No." *I'm already here.*

"If you're trying to give me a taste of my own medicine, it's working. I hated it when I didn't hear from you." She sniffled.

Is she crying? "Reina?" He stood, and the phone smashed into his cheekbone. "Ow! Shit."

"Ow? You were fighting, weren't you? Are you okay?" She

sucked in a breath. "At one of those mafia fights?"

"I didn't say that."

"You better not be. Damn it, now I'm getting upset."

"You don't get to be mad at me. I'm mad at you!"

"You have every right to be. But I couldn't stand it if you used your anger with me as an excuse for your reckless behavior. Those places are dangerous."

"I'm fine." Enjoying her concern and anger a little too much, he didn't bother to explain he'd been at the gym. Let her feel this fucked-up feeling for a while. It wasn't fun.

"You know, Brynn told me where you fight." Her voice lowered and took on a tone he couldn't quite identify. "She went to one of them when Alexei was fighting."

"Oh yeah?" Fear crept in, sitting square on his chest.

"Yeah. Since you think it's no big deal, maybe I need to go watch one of those fights myself."

"No. Absolutely. *Not*. Not going to happen."

"You're not the boss of me."

What the fuck?

"You better not step *one foot* in that place. Do you hear me?" *Coño.* He slammed his hand against the bike handle. "I can't believe you'd even think about doing something that stupid."

"You're the stupid one, fighting for the mob. You're putting yourself in danger, but I can't go and watch?"

"It's too dangerous! Promise me you'll never go."

"No."

"No?"

"The only way you can guarantee I never go...is to never fight there. Ever again!"

"Who *are* you? Where's the sweet girl who was too afraid to talk to a bunch of losers at speed dating?"

"I wasn't afraid. I lead a complicated life. I'm worried about you. And I don't want to be responsible for you getting hurt." Her voice broke, and it made his heart ache with remembered pain.

Today had been absolute shit.

"Reina, you ignored me all day long. You can't—It messes with my head. Takes me to a dark place. I told you about Rosie. I... Fighting is the only way for me to feel sane when I feel like this."

Now of all times, she decided to stay silent.

"You scared the shit out of me today!" The words came bursting through. "I'm not trying to control you or tell you what to do. My family says that shit all the time, but I'm not. I get worried. I swear to God, I want to know you're safe. That's it. I trusted you..."

With my heart. Fuck, he couldn't say that out loud. She'd run as fast as she could.

"But I didn't trust you in return. Is that what it felt like?"

"Yes."

"Theo, come inside."

"What?"

"Come inside. I know you're outside. I'm looking at you from my window."

"How'd you know?"

"When you yelled, our conversation echoed." She paused for a long time. "I trust you. Let me show you how much. Come inside."

"Only if you promise to tell me why you didn't call."

"The door's unlocked. Come in."

Chapter 26

SNACK TIME

REN WAITED AND watched. Minutes ticked by, and she hung up the phone, knowing that there wasn't anything more to say. She let her curtain drop and walked to her bathroom. She wore a cotton tank top and flannel short-shorts. He'd seen every inch of her, except for one part of her body.

He'd never seen her without a wig.

Ren looked over at her closet and saw the rainbow of hair sitting on wig stands. It would only be a few minutes to throw one on without a hair net and glue. It might not be as secure as she wanted, but she didn't need long to explain.

But she wouldn't. Tonight wasn't about her. She'd ruined the fragile trust that had grown between them, but she wanted to acknowledge what she'd done.

Please come in and talk to me.

Most people thought her wild wigs made her brave and bold, but they were her armor. Her protection against judgment. Her beautiful shield against the physical reminder of her autoimmune disease.

Tonight, she would show Theo who she really was. Fear had her hands shaking as she wrapped her head in a bright yellow scarf, the one she wore most nights after removing her hair. A deep sense of relief ran through her as she heard him tap at the door.

Rushing over, she threw it open and soaked him in. He was leaning against her doorframe, his helmet palmed in one big hand. The deepest, darkest frown sat right between his eyes. Eyes that looked filled with pain… and desolation.

He ran his gaze over every inch of her, only pausing briefly on her scarf. True to form, he didn't comment. Only waited.

"Come in, please." When he walked into the foyer, she saw his face under the bright light. "Oh, my God. You have *two black eyes?*" She grabbed his hand and tugged him inside, dropping his helmet on a side table before she led him into her kitchen. "I knew it. I knew you were fighting."

"Reina."

"Don't Reina me." She threw open the freezer and pulled out a packet of peas. "You make me so mad." She socked him in the shoulder. "*Ow.*"

He grabbed her hand and kissed her bruised knuckles. "I didn't."

Air rushed out of her lungs. The gentle pressure of his full lips affected her, making her instantly wet. Her whole body was sensitized to his every action. She tried to remember what they were talking about. "You didn't what?"

"Fight for *la mafia.*" He dropped her hand and stepped back, as if regretting the action.

"You didn't?" She stepped closer and pressed the peas against his eye, holding it there. "Then how'd this happen?"

"I fought at Tommy's gym." He winced when she pressed the packet a little harder.

"Sorry. Well, that's better, I guess?" She led him to her living room, not bothering to turn on any lights. The moon was strong tonight, filtering through the gauzy curtains framing her French doors. It illuminated her crystal table, each unique color highlighted by the soft glow. "But you're supposed to smash *them*. Remember?"

He looked down, obviously not ready to joke.

"I want to tell you what happened today. Sit." She sat on her plush couch and patted the cushion next to her, pretending not to notice the distance between them. "It isn't an excuse, but it's the truth." She cleared her throat, not used to him being so reserved. He usually touched her non-stop, making her feel secure and... cherished.

Damn, I'm messing this up. Here goes nothing. "I saw my ex to-day."

His head snapped up. "*What?*"

She nodded and squeezed his hand.

"Blue said to be patient." He gazed at the ceiling, as if he couldn't bear to look at her.

His actions felt like a knife to the heart. But it told her how much she'd hurt him. She made her voice light as she responded, "Blue's a smart man." She took a deep breath and rushed on. "I went to see my ex at a skilled nursing facility. Today is the anniversary of Nicholas' motorcycle accident. I always meet his mom at the facility to see him."

He blinked a few times and lowered the frozen peas. "I'm sorry, Reina."

"That's why I told you I'd lost someone too. Although, my circumstances are a little different. I know I'm lucky that I still get to see him, but it's...hard." She felt the silent tears slide down her cheeks, but she ignored them. She was so sick of the tears.

He sat there, his large frame swallowing her couch. "But why couldn't you text me? Tell me you were busy? After last night..." His deep voice sounded gruff.

"You're right. I hate that I did that. I don't want you to think I don't trust you or care about you."

"You'd have told me if you trusted me."

Is he right? "It all happened so fast between us..." His head snapped up, and she held up a hand to continue. "But you're right. I'm protective of him and his family. I wasn't ready to reveal everything. I avoided you because I didn't want to talk about it. That was the complicated part I mentioned during speed dating."

"Why not tell me?"

"That's a lot to hit someone with after a few days. All of this is moving so fast."

"When you know, you know." He stood and shouted, "Why am I the only one who understands this?"

He looked so pouty she couldn't fight the smile spreading across her face. She loved it when the tough Cuban emoted. She tugged him back down and brushed away a flake of ice on his cheek. "Oh yeah, what do you know?"

"Don't joke about this." He pounded his chest. "I know what I feel. I don't run away from it. And I don't hurt people I…"

"Care about?" she asked, fisting her hands, touched at the deepest part of her by his words. "You're right. When you know, you know. That's how I feel about you."

His hazel gaze beamed through her. "But you didn't tell me everything."

"I didn't. And it's still really messy. I am irrevocably tied to my ex. I always will be." She looked down at their hands, watching his thumb coast across the top of her palm. It was only a bit of affection, but it gave her hope. Maybe he was softening. "When I told you I wanted to give this a chance, I meant it."

"You did?"

"I did. But…"

"Fuck, I hate that word."

"Your reaction today was over the top. I feel like there's way more to it than you're sharing. Even though you said 'you know,' this is all new to me. I don't want to disappoint you, but you also can't expect me to act the way you want. I don't mind checking in, but I'm a grown woman who makes her own decisions. I'm not going to ask you for your permission if I want to go somewhere." It was crucial he understand this. More so than even mentioning Rosie and his shrine to her.

One step at a time.

"I know that! I swear, I do. But I don't know how much I can adjust. My head… it's not screwed on straight."

"I think your head is beautiful. Meet me halfway. I promise to be more communicative, but you can't assume the worst."

"I can…try?" He ran a hand down his face.

"You asking or telling?"

"It's hard to teach an old dog new tricks." He shook his head. "I can't make any promises. But I want to because…I'd do anything for you, Reina. Anything."

This was new to both of them, so she didn't push. There were still so many things to talk about, but they all flew away as she watched his hazel gaze ignite. His wicked grin appeared, the one that tilted up the right side of his mouth.

"This is pretty." He fingered the scarf draped over her shoulder, playing with the edge in his non-stop release of pent-up energy.

"It's a lot cooler than wearing a wig all the time. They get hot." She took a deep breath. "And it's my protection."

"Against who? Me?" The killer frown reappeared, front and center.

"Against the world. It hurt me when you thought I didn't trust you. I want to show you you're wrong. But I'm not going to lie, I'm a little freaked out about it. Which is pissing me off because I'm supposed to be beyond this."

"Tell me why you're freaked out." He grabbed her hand.

"I've worked hard to accept who I am." She looked down. "I'm mad at myself for hesitating now."

"Why? You don't feel safe with me?"

Those words broke her into tiny pieces and fundamentally shifted her perspective. It gave her an insight into the man he presented to the world, and who he really was.

He was worried she didn't feel safe. That was the one thing between them that had never been in doubt. Theo had made her feel cherished and protected from the moment they spoke. Even before they'd ever met, he'd defended her honor at a volleyball game.

"I *always* feel safe with you. That's why I want you to see the real me. Just me without anything to hide behind." Her hand shook as she pulled the scarf from her head. The hair she had left was about an inch long because she hadn't shaved it in a couple of months. Too short for the curl to pop, the dark-brown strands lay flat against her scalp. Right now, she was missing most of the hair on the right side of her head, and there was a smaller bald patch above her neck.

She wore no makeup, no fun scarves to distract—just the real her… and a shaky smile.

Theo cocked his head to the side and ran his intense gaze over her face. His big hand came up and lightly grasped her chin, tilting her head forward so he could see the sides and back of her head, intently studying her.

He palmed her head, rubbing it slowly, running the back of his fingers down her face and neck, lightly massaging her, and finally bringing his gaze back to hers. He smiled and leaned forward, nuzzling her head, kissing her temples, her ears, her bald spots. He lingered on each area, showing her love through each soft touch, eventually moving back to her face and peppering kisses over her eyelids that were leaking tears.

"You look beautiful, Reina. Like you always do. I see *you*. That's all I've ever seen."

She nodded, unable to speak. She believed him.

With a soft tug, he positioned her in his lap. She collapsed into his arms, letting the tears purge her of uncertainty and fear. His big arms banded around her and held her while she cried. The culmination of their fight, the realization she would have to confront

Señora Gonzalez, and the fact that she'd hurt Theo poured out of her. Even though she'd messed up, he still held her.

Theo's unwavering support helped her release the need to hold back. She'd known that it didn't matter what others thought about her, but she'd also numbed her own feelings by not letting people in. People like Theo Romero. She couldn't completely blame her lack of dating and relationships on Nicholas's accident. Another part of it had been her way of protecting herself from the pain of loss.

"Reina, I love you in my arms." He tilted her face back and kissed her, coaxing her to part her lips.

With a moan, she allowed his thick tongue inside her mouth, wallowing in the pure pleasure of sharing soft sighs and wet lips. Then she felt it, the tongue piercing that brought her so much pleasure, rolling against her tongue, reminding her of every time he'd claimed her sex, ensuring total bliss. "I want to see you this time. I want to watch you come."

"You do?" He rocked against her, and they both moaned.

"I think you're beautiful. I love your body." Ren straddled him and ground against his rock-hard erection.

"What'll you give me for it?"

She thought about it. It had to be something good because she really wanted to see this man move. When inspiration hit, a broad smile crept over her face. "What is the very first thing you asked me to do for you? The first night together at the gym?"

"To go down on you? To devour you with my mouth and tongue. For you to give me a taste of that milk and honey? While you read your manual." He cocked a brow and instead of making her laugh, she felt soaked between her thighs. Because she was remembering every swipe of his pierced tongue.

"Yes." She moaned and sat back. "And I let you. But what else did you want?"

His lids went heavy. "You were so shy, I didn't get a chance to ask you to touch yourself. I wanted to see how you made yourself feel good."

"You do it for me. I'll do it for you." Her cheeks, neck, and chest all felt hot, like a full-body blush.

Theo Romero, black-eyed hottie, stood and whipped off his shirt. "If you put on some reggaeton, I could give you a real show." He started dancing, grinding his hips, spinning in place, each piece of clothing stripped to an imaginary beat. But right before his pants came off, he stopped.

"Don't stop," she said breathlessly.

"I want you naked." He waved his hand over her body. "And I want to see you touch yourself while I strip."

"But then I might close my eyes." Pleasure pooled between her thighs. She'd be surprised if she hadn't soaked her pajamas. That thought would have sent her into convulsions not long ago, dead with embarrassment. But now she wanted him to see her. He'd convinced her he loved it.

"Nope. You're going to keep your eyes right here." He unzipped his jeans, his thick cock protruding over his boxer briefs, gently slapping his lower stomach. The mushroom head resting against his belly button.

"Devastatingly sexy." Her lids went heavy, but she didn't dare close her eyes. She wanted to see this beautiful man take himself in hand. She whipped off her top, relishing his groan as he watched her boobs bounce for him. She squeezed them together, and he lunged but she held him off with one hand. "You're obsessed with my boobs."

"I am!"

"I know. I love it." She arched her back even as she held him back. He growled, but she said, "If you start kissing me, I won't touch myself for you. I want to see you this time. *Please.* I know it will be so beautiful."

"You talked me into it," he grumbled. Kicking off his boots and shoving down his pants in seconds, he turned around to place them out of the way, giving her a glance of his amazing ass.

She decided it was her turn to shock him, so she stripped down as quickly as possible. By the time he spun back, she'd placed her heels on the couch, her legs spread wide, giving him a full view of her world.

"*Reina.*" He stumbled and stepped forward.

"I'm so wet for you." She ran her hand down her belly, between her thighs. He'd wrung so much pleasure from her these past few days, she felt like a different woman. All of her insecurities about him watching her, gone. Because of his focused care. Because of his talented tongue.

He looked shell-shocked.

"Do you want me to stop?" She paused, her fingers just above her dewy lips.

"No." He grabbed his cock, gliding his hand from base to tip.

She watched, fascinated with the way he handled himself, snapping his wrist at the end, almost pinching the tip. She sat up to get a better view. "Is that how you want me to touch you? Rough like that?"

His head fell back, but he kept his eyes on her. "I want you any way I can have you. Your turn. Get to it." He kicked up his chin, and she looked down at her plump lips, so tender and red for him.

"I forgot." She wanted this. Wanted him to see her. No more fear or shyness. She lightly ran her forefinger over her throbbing clit, coating it in her silky juices that wet her thighs. "I'm so ready for you."

"Can't wait to feel you." He squeezed harder, jerking his cock faster and faster. "Love your eyes on me. Addicted to the way you look at me."

She loved the pull and sway of heavy muscles as he took control. And his piercings! That man had far too many sexy attributes. She brushed her folds with her fingers, circling her clit as pleasure bracketed her, taking her to the edge. All she could see, think about, was his fat cock. And she wanted it. Now. She fingered herself a little faster, a little harder. She needed to come, and she wanted to do it while he watched her.

I want to show him.

"You look so sexy, *mi Reina*. Fuck, I want you so bad."

"It feels so good. I want more," she cried out.

"Come for me. Let me see you." His big hand trailed down to heavy balls and tugged forcefully. "See what you do to me."

"Theo, I want you inside of me. I want to come feeling you right here…" She plunged a finger into her hot sheath and arched her back, crying out. "I'm so close."

"Holy shit, you look so hot. Let me get a condom." He rifled around his jeans and grabbed his wallet. "Wait for me, baby."

"But it feels so good." Her fingers rolled her clit faster. "I need you. I'm so wet. Look."

"I have to taste you." He fell to his knees.

"Yes!" His thick tongue replaced her hand, one of his long fingers piercing her at the same time. Her inner muscles clenched around him and she cried out, "Yes, yes! I'm there. Just like that. Right there!" She came, one of the most powerful orgasms of her life, the pleasure arrowing between her legs and spiraling out, washing her body in searing ecstasy.

He lapped her sensitive clit, nice and slow, right through her orgasm. "Beautiful. I want to see it again."

"Please, baby. I want to feel close to you. Come inside me." She watched as he slid on the condom and tugged at her thighs, positioning her at the edge of the couch.

He came up on his knees and placed his hard dick at her entrance, coating his cock in her juices. His thick head teased her, the tip entering her and then pulling out, his neck muscles taut and strained. "Turns me on."

How had he lasted this long? She already felt on edge, and she'd just come. Whimpering, she threw her hands above her head, submitting to the pleasure—ceding total control.

He leaned over and grasped one of her breasts, circling the globe, squeezing it until her nipples puckered. He opened his mouth and enclosed her areola as he plunged inside her, rolling the tip between his teeth. "So fucking good!" He roared around her breasts as he moved his hips, pounding into her over and over.

Ren smiled as her orgasm reignited and grew. She'd never experienced anything like it. Her inner walls gripped his thick shaft in increasing degrees, milking and loving this powerful man.

Her breast popped out of his mouth and he leaned against her, twining his fingers in hers above her head. "I don't ever want this to end."

She licked up his neck, sucking and kissing as he pistoned inside of her, his defined glutes flexing with each deep thrust.

He slammed a hand against her waist, pummeling her and adding the extra friction of his piercing to her throbbing clit.

"*Yes.*" The pleasure built, about to explode. "Yes!"

"Reina." He breathed as his body dug in one last time, and froze, the muscle in his cheek pulsing as he stirred his cock in her, extending his orgasm. "Can feel you gripping me!" he shouted as his head reared back, his last thrust sending her over the edge, ecstasy building from her core and spiraling out until she felt it to the tips of her toes.

He collapsed on top of her, his heaving chest scraping her sensitive nipples, extending her pleasure, igniting a mini orgasm that made her gasp.

Eventually, their breaths stilled, and she looked around, laughing softly.

"What?"

"What is it with us and couches?" She ruffled his hair, loving how deliciously rumpled he looked.

"Not my fault you look so sexy." He ruined his sweet words with a giant yawn.

"Right." She kissed his lips softly, floored that he genuinely meant it. As if she were the sexy one in the relationship. "I think we're ready to move to the next step in our relationship." His head popped up. "Take me to a real bed. I think we've earned it."

Chapter 27

68 (I'LL OWE YOU ONE)

FRIDAY

*B*AM! *BAM! BAM!*

Ren woke with a start, looking around in a panic. All she saw was Theo's big body sprawled around hers. She peeked out between his arms, gazing at his beautiful face, completely relaxed and at peace. Maybe she could sneak a—

Bam!

There it was again. Someone was pounding on her front door. And of course, Theo was oblivious. Deepest sleeper ever. Untangling herself from his arms, she grabbed her pajama shorts and top. Everything was covered, but in the light of day her pajamas felt very thin. With no time to put on her scarf, she grabbed a baseball cap, the one she kept by the front door for emergencies. Tiptoeing over to the peephole, she gasped when she saw her mother-in-law standing on the other side of the door.

No, not my mother-in-law. Señora Gonzalez, my ex's mother. Shit. Shit, shit, shit.

Unwilling to be completely disrespectful by ignoring the woman, she cracked open the door. "Señora, is everything okay?"

"No, *mija*. It's not. I want to talk to you about Nicholas and those terrible doctors. You're the only one they listen to." She pressed a hand to her forehead. "*Dios mío*. I'm not happy with the facility anymore. We need to move him as soon as possible."

Not again. Ren shut her eyes briefly. This would be the second move this year alone. The logistics of it were a nightmare. One of the nurses or doctors must have alluded to the fact that Nicholas had no more brain activity and wouldn't come out of the coma. They may have even advised her to remove all life support.

"*Well?* Let me in. This is an emergency!" She fanned her cheeks, her face and neck covered in sweat.

"Señora, are you okay?"

"I'm fine."

"Um... well, now isn't a good time. Why don't I meet you at the nursing facility tomorrow? I have to teach a class tonight but..."

"A class? On what? You aren't a teacher." She pulled at her shirt, fanning her breast. "What's this class about."

"Oh..." Ren cleared her throat. "This and that." *Please Theo, please stay asleep.*

"Why aren't you letting me in. Do you have," she gasped, "*company?*" Her shrewd eyes moved over her sleepwear, which suddenly felt extremely skimpy. She lifted up on tiptoe to look over Ren's shoulder.

Oh hell, if ever there were ever a time when she needed to come up with the perfect lie, it was now. But when Ren opened her mouth, "Yes," slipped out. Lying to herself, she rated at championship level. But lying to someone she loved, to their face after they asked a direct question? She couldn't do it.

"A *man?*"

"Señora, please. I tried to talk to you about this yesterday—"

"Reina. Where the hell are you?" Theo called from the bedroom.

Now he wakes up? Of all times.

Señora Gonzalez pushed her way inside and pointed at Theo, who looked deliciously rumpled, standing in her living room in nothing but black boxer briefs. "You're cheating on my beautiful son with *him?*"

Theo blinked, his hand freezing on his muscular chest. At least he'd thrown something on. "Cheating?"

"You're engaged to my son! And to leave when he's fighting for his life?" Tears gathered in the woman's dark eyes. "No! I won't allow it. I won't!"

"Engaged?" Theo rumbled.

Ren ignored Theo and watched Señora Gonzalez rail against Theo, and against Ren, and her life. It was all extremely painful and over the top. *Something's wrong.* "Please, Señora. Come sit down. I can explain…"

"You better mean to *me*. Not him." Señora Gonzalez crossed her arms.

Ren sighed. "Nicholas and I were never engaged. Let's take a minute to sit down and talk this out. Theo was on his way out." Ren pleaded with him with her eyes. He had to understand that Señora Gonzalez was her first priority.

"And what is *this?*" Señora Gonzalez walked over to Theo's helmet and spun around, tears streaming down her face. "He rides one of these death machines?" Her voice barely above a whisper. "You know what they've taken from me."

"I know." Ren had no defense. "But please, I would never want to hurt you. If we can talk this out, I'm sure you'll understand what's happening."

"I understand perfectly." She tugged at her clothes, pacing the room. "You want to leave my baby. *He'll be all alone.*"

"Señora, what—"

"Did you ride?" Señora Gonzalez spun around and got in Theo's face, pointing at his chest. "With him?"

175

Ren's world spun, guilt eating away at her. She had no defense. She never expected to ride a motorcycle again. But she'd trusted Theo and believed him when he'd said the accident shouldn't define her or make her live in fear. All of this pain was her fault for avoiding the truth and trying to protect Señora Gonzalez's feelings. "Yes, I did."

"Get out." Señora Gonzalez grabbed the helmet and shoved it into Theo's arms. "*Sal de aquí*! Now! Go away!"

"Engaged?" Theo repeated, still struck dumb as he grabbed the helmet.

"Yes. She is an *engaged* woman. To my son. Haven't you been listening?" Señora Gonzalez sobbed into her hands, and Ren ran to get some tissue. "What will I do?"

As Ren passed Theo, she whispered, "You better go."

He paused, his wide chest expanding, refusing to look at her. After a few weighted seconds, he scooped up his clothes and stormed out.

"I'll be right back, Señora."

"What? No! You're leaving with—"

Ren gently closed the door on the Señora's wide eyes, shutting her own for a minute as she processed what had happened. And what she'd have to face. But it was long overdue. In a few moments, she and Nicholas' mother would have the talk they should have had years ago.

"Engaged?" Theo called out to her as he hooked a leg over his bike. "I'd never believe it, but I've asked you three times and you're not denying it."

Ren followed, shaking her head when she saw the fury etched on his face. *Unbelievable.* "I don't have time to explain, but you have to know I'm not engaged."

"Then what the hell is that?" He waved a hand at her front door, shoving his legs in his pants and slipping on his shoes. "What the hell is she talking about?"

"That's a grieving mother who lost her son. Who's not ready to let go—of him or anyone that's connected to him. And for a few years, I did the same." She stood in front of the bike, ignoring the nosy neighbor who stared out her window. "But not anymore. I'm going to explain everything. And I was never engaged."

"But why doesn't *she* know that? And why didn't you tell me about it last night? We were telling each other everything." He palmed his helmet.

"Theo, I promise you, I will fix this. All of it. But right now, I'm worried about her. This reaction is too much, even for her. I think something else is going on." She sighed and walked over to him. "Please, can you give me a little time?"

He paused and looked at her window. Señora Gonzalez blatantly stared at them through the curtains. He shook his head. "I'll leave. But you're calling me."

"Yes. I will. I promise."

"No repeat of yesterday. That shit messes with me."

"I know." She lifted a hand but paused because Nicholas' mom was still staring. Ren had been taught to respect her elders and couldn't make out with Theo in front of her. The whole situation was a giant mess. And all her fault. "I'll talk to you later." She turned back to the door.

"You're walking away from me?" Theo's mouth dropped open.

Because he communicated so much through touch, Ren understood he'd feel like this was a slap in the face. But she didn't have a choice. Señora Gonzalez needed her. "Yes. But I'll call you later. Bye."

Theo slammed on his helmet and sped off far faster than she would have liked. But Ren made a conscious effort to put him out of her mind. Grasping the door handle, she was shocked to see Señora Gonzalez crumpled on her couch. She rushed over. "Are you all right? What is going on?"

"He'll be all alone. All alone." She pierced Ren with her dark eyes. "You were the only one I trusted. To take care of him."

"What do you mean? I'll always help with Nicholas. You know that. You know me." She sat next to her and rubbed her back. "And he has you. The most dedicated mother I know. He's so lucky to——"

"I'm dying." She wiped tears from her cheeks. "I've started chemotherapy. That's why I'm sweating like this. My prognosis… is not good." She shook her head. "Who will take care of *mi bebé?* What will he do when he wakes up all alone? I'll be gone. And you'll be with *him*." She gestured at the window, indicating Theo.

"I'm so sorry to hear this." Ren's hands trembled as she took the frail woman's palms in her own. "I swear to you, Señora. I will always look after Nicholas. Always. It doesn't matter who I'm dating."

"How could you have changed your mind for that *maniac?* Tattoos and muscles. He looked like a convict! I saw that giant death machine. You're leaving my boy all alone." She wailed into her hands. "You were engaged!"

"Señora, you know that's not true. We were never engaged. Nicholas and I were kids. In our first year of college. We were growing apart, but I loved him from the first day I met him. I still do. That will *never* change." She sniffled, shoving her own feelings of loss deep down inside. Señora Gonzalez had been prickly and demanding but still an important mother figure to Ren. That was why she hadn't wanted to hurt her. "Now, tell me about your treatments. I want to hear everything." Ren held her and listened, silently vowing to do everything in her power to help them.

Chapter 28

VJ NOT A BJ

R EN MOVED LIKE an automaton through her shift at the hospital. She'd agreed to work a few hours, so she'd have plenty of time to get ready for the class tonight. It all seemed so silly now. In the grand scheme of things, her worries over teaching and talking about cunnilingus all seemed ridiculous. But she would suck it up and perform. Like she always did.

Theo had texted a few times, and she'd dutifully responded. Not long texts, but enough to let him know she'd call as soon as she had a minute. The morning had been overwhelming, dealing with patients and calling every pancreatic specialist she knew. The more she learned about the diagnosis, the more resigned she became.

On top of all of that, she had to find a new home for Nicholas. Señora Gonzalez had thoroughly burned her bridges at the current facility, and Ren needed to figure out a way to get Nicholas in somewhere that didn't have a yearlong waitlist *and* accepted Medicare.

Ping.

Theo again: Call me.

It was time to talk, but she was avoiding it. His surly attitude, even though *he knew* she wasn't engaged, rubbed her raw. Usually, when he became pouty, she thought it was cute, but right now she was out of patience. Although maybe it wasn't fair to judge him. He'd received a pretty big shock.

She sighed and dialed his number.

"You okay?" he asked.

"I'm a little overwhelmed." Silence sat between them and Ren hated it. "Are you mad?"

"No. *Yes.* I've been waiting to hear from you and get an explanation about what the hell happened."

"I know." She sat in an empty waiting room, tucking her foot under her thigh. "Sorry. I was making arrangements for Nicholas, and time got away from me. Can we talk in person? I want to get out of here, take a shower, and get over to the school to prep for the class."

"Fuck the class. I need answers. Why does that woman feel like you're engaged to her son?"

"Theo, I know it must have been a shock, but you know the circumstances. I didn't want to hurt her feelings. Her son is in a coma." Ren lowered her voice. "Why are you yelling at me?"

"Because you're pulling away." He growled into the phone. "I'm getting a pit in my stomach just like the other day when you ghosted me."

"I did not." She rubbed her temples. "Okay, yes I did, but this isn't the same."

"Then tell me. What else is going on? You're acting differently."

Ren hesitated to share with him. This was her responsibility, *her* family to fix. Theo had his own issues to work through; she didn't want to pile more onto him. No, that wasn't true. Even after their amazing night together, they'd never addressed his Rosie shrine. His attachment to his ex made her wary. Maybe he wasn't ready to move on. Maybe she needed to be a bit more honest and admit she didn't want to share Señora Gonzalez's diagnosis with him.

For someone used to handling everything by herself, things had progressed way too quickly with Theo. She'd spent the last few years alone. Now he wanted her to tear herself open, when he hadn't done the same.

"You see. You're cutting me out. Again." His voice dropped. "You should've been clear with that woman. She can't expect you to remain engaged to him."

"I was *never* engaged. Why aren't you being more understanding about the situation?"

A loud bang reverberated through the phone, as if he'd slammed a door shut. "Admit it. You didn't say anything because you're not ready to move on."

"You're kidding me, right?" Ren's anger didn't show often, but when her long fuse was lit, watch out. A good part of it was her fury at herself for not clearing things up, but Theo was in denial. He, of all people, shouldn't mention *anything* about moving on. Not with the way his house was decorated. "You need to ask yourself that."

"What the hell does that mean?"

"Have you seen your house? And you're right, we didn't talk about everything last night because once again, I didn't want to hurt anyone's feelings. *Your* feelings." She took a deep breath and rushed on, "When I woke up after spending the night at your house, I was freaked out."

"About what?" His voice sounded deceptively soft, but she could feel his ire.

"Your house is a shrine to Rosie."

"I don't—What do you mean?"

"Theo, there are pictures, and paintings... and handwritten notes. Everywhere!"

"You're upset about a few pictures? Those were gifts people gave me. What else was I supposed to do with them? Get rid of them?" He growled. "I can't do that to her."

"That's why I didn't mention it. But we're both navigating our losses and apparently not doing a very good job of it." She looked at her watch, realizing she needed to head home and shower. *Now.* The class was only a few hours away. "You better ask yourself the same things you're asking me."

"You let a woman believe you were engaged to her son."

"Yes, I did." She rubbed her forehead, bone tired. "But I told her the truth yesterday, and it was difficult because… I hurt her." She gulped in air. "But it was the right thing to do. I made a deep cut to a woman who has lived in pain for years. Are you ready to do the same?"

"I'm not the one who lied!"

"I was trying to protect her." She clenched the phone in her hand. "You know what, you didn't lie but you tell half-truths or avoid things, don't you? You know I worry about you fighting, but you've never said you'll stop. You came to my house with two black eyes! You told me you could quit if you want, that there's nothing holding you there. Yet you haven't made the decision. Why?"

Dead silence, and for a moment she thought he'd hung up until he said, "It helps me clear my head."

"Clear your head from what? From Rosie?" She winced, knowing she'd gone too far but having to add, "You obviously don't want to talk about her. I get it. Believe me, *I get it.* We're both tethered to our pasts. But you can't judge me for holding on too long, too."

"This is seriously fucked up. Why is everything so hard with you?" He revved the engine, like he was about to get on his bike and head out.

Ren gripped the phone, her stomach dropping with each passing second. "You know it freaks me out every time you get on that bike. Don't speed off mad. If you still want to, we'll talk after class. But I have to help my mother-in-law… I mean my ex's mom." *Shit. Wrong thing to say.*

"*Mother-in-law?* Exactly." He revved the bike again. "People have a habit of disappointing me. I thought you were different. I'm out."

Ren could barely breathe, her chest tight with pain. He was petulant and behaving like a toddler because he was hurt. But the rational part of her was not in control right now. He was going to kill himself, and it would be her fault.

History may repeat itself, and there was nothing she could do to stop it.

Chapter 29

SCUBA DIVING

REN PARKED IN the back of the charm school and sat for a moment as she collected herself. *Pull it together, girl. You have a class to teach!* With a shaky hand, she adjusted the rearview mirror to check her makeup. Her red bangs framed her chiffon lashes and makeup. Everything was on point. She should have looked amazing, but all she saw were glassy eyes and pale skin.

I'm a mess.

She couldn't get Theo off her mind, convinced he'd hurt himself because of their argument. Then the rational part of her brain would kick in and chastise herself for thinking she could control the world. If Theo wanted to drive like a maniac, that was *his* choice. Plus, he had seriously pissed her off. His response felt so selfish to her.

But you didn't tell him what was really going on, a tiny, annoying voice whispered. Regret had started to creep in. Why couldn't she open up completely to him? Didn't he deserve better?

Please be safe, she repeated on a loop every few minutes.

Frustrated, she reached across and scooped up her bag filled with VJ accoutrements. Luckily, she made it to the school with time to spare, even after everything that had gone down.

Her connection to Señora Gonzalez had strengthened. They were united in their love for Nicholas. Their talk gave her the opportunity, engaged or not, to reassure her of her commitment to him. It would never wane. If something did happen to his mother, she would always take care of Nicholas.

Hiking her bag over her shoulder, Ren wobbled on her high-heeled boots as she made her way through the backdoor. Checking her phone for the thousandth time, she sighed. Still nothing from Theo. She couldn't bring herself to reach out to him, still in disbelief about their argument. If she called him, she wouldn't even know where to begin, her emotions a jumbled mix of worry, guilt, and anger. And then he'd rushed off on his bike.

The worry was killing her.

Rounding the corner, she was surprised to see the school was popping. A set-up crew raced around, unfolding white chairs and arranging them in the large ballroom. Twinkling lights hung from the vaulted ceilings, complimenting the mint green walls and strategically placed hydrangeas. Straight from Ms. Belle's garden.

"Ren, you're here." Ms. Hattie walked over, leaning heavily on her cane. She enveloped her in a giant hug. After a few good squeezes, she pulled back and cupped her cheeks. "What's the matter, baby? Are you all right?"

"I'm a little nervous about teaching the class."

"It's more than that." Ms. Hattie shook her head, her tight gray curls not moving an inch. "Come and sit down with The Ladies and Henry. We'll help you get to the bottom of whatever's bothering you. We have hundreds of years' experience between the three of us." She winked.

"Thank you, Ms. Hattie. You're always so thoughtful." Ren hugged her again, loving the unique combination of Jean Naté and cinnamon that surrounded the happy octogenarian. "Is Brynn doing okay?"

"Yes. Alexei spent the night, refusing to let her get up for a thing. He even carried her to the ladies' room. Such an attentive boy. He's going to be a wonderful father." She patted Ren's hand and led her to Brynn's room.

"I wasn't planning on speaking with Brynn, Ms. Hattie. I wanted to make sure she was feeling well." Ren felt bad about burdening Brynn again. She'd already spoken to her about Theo yesterday, and now things were even worse between them.

"Nonsense." Hattie hustled her along with surprising speed. She tapped on the door but immediately walked in, announcing with dramatic glee, "We have an emergency." Clearly, Brynn and Alexei were not expecting the interruption and were *comiendo pan delante los pobres.* "We're not interrupting, are we?" Ms. Hattie nudged Ren with her elbow and giggled.

"No, of course not. What's the emergency?" Brynn reached over to the nightstand, grabbed her glasses, and rammed them onto her nose. "What happened?"

Alexei calmly unfurled his large body from the bed, kissed Brynn, and then sauntered over to Ren. "Thanks for taking care of my angel." He wrapped her up in a big hug, even lifting her off her feet.

Stunned, Ren hugged him back, not used to such emotion from the aloof artist. He kept his distance from most people besides Brynn... and Theo. "I can't take any of the credit. The Ladies were amazing and stayed with her most of the time." She lifted a shaky hand to her fire-engine red wig.

"Where's Theo?"

"I don't know." Her eyes watered for a second, but she blinked it away. The last few days had opened the floodgates. She hadn't cried this much since...well, yesterday and frequently before that. Because, yes, she was a crier, but even for her this was too much. Besides, she was mad and had no time for tears. "I probably shouldn't talk to you guys about it again. I can't keep running to you every time we have an argument."

"Get used to it. Theo's a lot," Alexei said.

"Alexei." Brynn laughed.

"What?" He smiled, and it transformed his already handsome face into perfection. "It's true."

"I knew something was wrong." Hattie wrapped her arm around Ren's waist and walked her over to Brynn so she could sit on the bed. "What did that stubborn boy do?"

Ren sighed. "We fought again this morning. Maybe we expected too much from each other."

"Don't worry. Henry and I are here." Ms. Scarlett rushed through like a pink tornado, dragging in a white poster board, the kind used for science projects.

"Oh, dear God. This is bad," Brynn whispered and grabbed Ren's hand. "Whatever you do, do *not* look directly at the board."

"Why not?" Ren couldn't resist and watched as Ms. Scarlett leaned the trifold against the wall, on full display. It was a massive, anatomically correct rendering of a woman's vagina along with arrows and name tags of the clitoris, labia, and oh so much more. It put Ren's simple diagrams to shame. "*Omigod.*"

"It's the instructional diagram I presented to Henry on our first date."

Old Henry lumbered in, and the whole room stared after him. He nodded and headed for his favorite chair, tucked in the corner of the room.

"Maybe we should let Brynn and Ren talk," Alexei said to the chatty octogenarians who were *oohing* and *aahing* over the chart.

"I would never leave my baby when she needs us." Hattie slapped his tattooed arm. "What happened with Theo? We must know."

Ren looked around the room, accepting this would be a group conversation. "We fought about our pasts, and how hard it is to let go of that pain."

"You've both gone through so much loss," Brynn whispered,

and squeezed her hand.

"I didn't handle everything as well as I should. I've made a lot of mistakes." Ren looked down at Brynn's hand gripping her own.

"What did you do, *mija*?" Ms. Babe asked as she and her sister pushed their way inside the room. It was official. The gang had arrived.

"I'm sure we can help." Ms. Nancy and her sister wore matching beehive hairdos.

"Where do I start? I feel bad, but I'm mad at him, too!" Surrounded by everyone, Ren felt loved but a bit suffocated. She wasn't used to this much maternal concern. "First of all, he keeps talking about me being engaged." The crowd gasped but Ren waved them off. "He *knows* I'm not."

"But why would he think that?" Ms. Scarlett asked. "Are you in an open relationship, dear? I hear that's all the rage. Right, Henry?"

Old Henry responded with a definitive thumbs-down.

"Oh dear, I forgot how ferociously jealous he can be." Scarlett walked over and patted his shoulder.

Old Henry had already dozed off.

"Go on, dear. You were explaining about your open relationship." Ms. Scarlett motioned her on.

"I'm not engaged or in an open relationship. I swear." She sighed, obviously not communicating well. "But I let my ex's mom think we were engaged because I didn't want to hurt her feelings." *This sounds bad.*

"Why would you put her feelings above your own?" Ms. Hattie asked.

"I..." That was an amazing question. "It's a long story, but you're right, Ms. Hattie. I shouldn't have done that." She looked around and they looked...scandalized. Except Ms. Scarlett. She looked intrigued. "It gets worse. When he called me on being fake-engaged, I lashed out about his ex-girlfriend and all the pictures he has of her at his house. I called it a shrine to Rosie."

More silence. Even Old Henry looked a bit shocked. Now that he was awake.

"Do you regret what you said?" Ms. Scarlett asked.

"Well, I didn't until I saw all your faces." She rooted around her purse and found her amethyst stone. She held tight, hoping for some serenity. "It's no excuse, but he was being so judgmental, saying I hadn't gotten over my ex. But *he's* still connected to his as well. There were a lot of pictures and paintings of her, but I hate how I said it. The bigger concern is whether he's ready to move on. Which is what he's been accusing me of, too." She sighed. "And now, I don't even know if I had the right to say anything. He'll probably never forgive me."

"He'll come around," Brynn said.

"You don't understand. I think he's done." Ren shook her head. "He called me a disappointment."

"What?" The Ladies gasped and clutched their pearls. "He didn't."

Alexei shook his head. "Don't worry. He says stupid shit he doesn't mean on a daily basis. It's his temper."

Brynn opened a side drawer and pulled out a giftbag. "I got you a thank you gift. I was going to give it to you after the class, but I think you could use it now."

Ren unwrapped it and gasped. Trail mix... and it was her favorite kind! She tore open the bag and poured it into her hands, picking out the essential bits. "Thanks. I feel better already." But that wasn't true. Now that the anger had faded, she missed Theo.

"How are we going to fix things? Get you two back on track? You're so good together. I saw it the other night, and I have a knack for predicting these things." Ms. Hattie accepted the offered trail mix and passed it around to the crowd.

The whole gang nodded in agreement.

"It's not even about me anymore, Ms. Hattie. He drove off on his motorcycle, and I'm worried he's going to do something reckless. I'm terrified he'll get hurt." Tears clouded her eyes again, but this time it was harder to blink them away.

"I'll find him." Alexei unfolded his crossed arms.

"Alexei will fix it." Brynn smiled at her man. "He'll know what to say." Brynn pulled out the tissues from the bedside table and handed them to Ren.

"What do you want me to tell him?" Alexei bent down and gave Brynn a scorching goodbye kiss.

"Tell him…" A million things flitted through her mind, but she returned to the same thought each time. "To please be safe. Don't do something stupid because of me."

"Knowing Theo, it's too late for that. But I'll try." Alexei grabbed his leather jacket and headed out the door.

Chapter 30

AUSSIE KISS

"SHADOW!" THEO SLAMMED the front door, refusing to look at any of the pictures lining his living room walls. He went straight into the spare bedroom, his makeshift gym, and fished around his closet for his gym bag. "Where the hell are you, dog?"

The house was empty. Even man's best friend was avoiding him. *Me vale verga! I don't give a shit.*

He didn't want to feel anymore, and he only ever had two ways to release the pain. Riding and fighting. Because of Reina and the sheer terror in her voice when they spoke, he'd parked the bike as soon as he'd gotten home. But he couldn't sit around and think about Rosie. It would bring back all the festering pain. The torture of not knowing night after night where she was, watching her and Alexei in the hospital, burned within an inch of their lives... It was too much to process.

Alexei had made it out; Rosie hadn't.

He stuffed his gym bag full of everything he needed: fighting shorts, open-fingered gloves, cup, and mouth guard. Heading out the front door, he ignored Reina's words that played on a loop. He hadn't walked away from fighting for *la mafia* because he needed the outlet. Racing down his front steps, he came face-to-face with his childhood friend and overall pain in the ass. "Fucking hell. What are you doing here?"

"Saving your ass. As usual." Alexei stood there, wide stance, with his stupid, pretty-boy smirk. Blocking his bike.

"Get the fuck out of my way."

"Nope."

Theo eyed Alexei. They'd trained together for years, knew each and every one of the other's weaknesses and strengths. If Theo started this fight, he didn't know how it would end. But he was already sizing him up, ready to take him on. Theo itched to connect his fist to something. Alexei's face was as good as anyone else's.

"Don't do it, man."

"*Cierra la puta boca!* You don't know what the hell you're talking about."

"The hell I don't. I know that look. You're about to do something really stupid."

"Bullshit. You have three seconds to move, or I do it for you." Theo stalked forward. "Brynn will be pissed if I kill you."

"I'm not moving."

"Fuck this."

Two seconds later they had their hands on their necks, grappling and wrestling on the grass of his front yard. It had been reflex—what they'd always done as kids. Wrestle rather than box so they wouldn't leave any marks and get in trouble with their families. His mom would scream for hours every time he came home with a shiner or a busted lip.

"Ren told me about your fight." Alexei grunted through the hold Theo had on his neck.

"So?" Theo's whole chest hurt thinking about the past few days. The engagement, the familiar pain etched on the face of Reina's ex's mother. He hadn't liked what Señora Gonzalez had said, but he recognized the kind of devastation that changed a person on a cellular level.

"I know you. You're about to do something you can't take back. Something Ren won't forgive you for. You're going to lose her." Alexei slapped him upside the head.

"Ow! Damn it! You aren't even taking this fight seriously." Theo hooked his foot behind Alexei's knees and pushed, sending Alexei flying. Theo took advantage of the seconds it took for his friend to get up and headed for his bike. He needed a real fight and didn't want to deliver pain to Alexei like he could to a total stranger.

"She's not engaged," Alexei said, standing slowly.

"I know that! I'm not an idiot." Theo palmed his helmet.

Alexei cocked his brow.

"Don't give me that fucking look. A lot happened that you don't know about."

"I spoke to her at the school."

"Why would she talk to you?" He blinked and stopped before he got on his bike. "Did something happen? Is she okay?"

"She's worried sick about your sorry ass. Why am I even telling you this? You don't care. You're going to end up fighting or wrecking on that bike, and you could lose her forever."

Theo raged, overcome with such fierce anger he couldn't breathe. Spiking his helmet on the floor, Theo walked over and kicked Alexei's leg. After all the shit he'd put him through, Alexei had the nerve to lecture *him*? "Doing something I'll regret? Like becoming a junkie like you?"

"Say it! Like me *and* Rosie. You've always been pissed at me for my drug abuse, and I deserved it. But you haven't processed your feelings about her. You never admit the anger. She was *an addict*." Alexei stood and stared him down. "Just like me."

"Don't talk about her like that!"

"Why not? She was my friend, too. I loved her. I understood her. She was sunshine and joy, but she had an abusive as hell father and a terrible disease. She wanted to escape. Like I did. Don't do that to her. Don't pretend that you didn't see all of her."

"Reina said… she said I have to get rid of all of her pictures."
Theo closed his eyes, beaten down by the rage and anger he held
for his beautiful Rosie. The girl who wouldn't hurt a fly, who always
kissed his hurts away.

"Ren said that?"

"No, maybe… I can't think." Theo couldn't breathe—his love
for Rosie mixed with sorrow. Alexei was wrong. He'd admitted his
anger for a while now. But getting rid of her stuff? Most of the
time, he didn't even see the pictures. The whole neighborhood had
brought them over after the funeral because they knew how much
he loved her. Theo's mom had arranged them around his house, so
they wouldn't sit in the spare room and gather dust. "Reina's
worried I haven't moved on. I have. But if I get rid of all her stuff,
she'll…"

"What?"

"Disappear."

"She won't, man. I bet her mom would love all of those pictures. And you don't have to get rid of everything. Come on."
Alexei grabbed him by the front of his T-shirt and dragged him into
the house, stopping short in front of the fireplace. "Shit. I haven't
been over here in a while. You have a *painting* of her on the mantel?
And what are all these letters and cards?"

Theo looked around and tried to see the place from Reina's
POV. "It might be… a lot."

"You think? I'll help you move the stuff to the van and then
we'll call her mom."

Theo picked up the photo of the three of them, from their
seventh grade beach trip. It had been the day he first declared his
undying love. Rosie had always been right there with him, the three
of them inseparable, until Alexei and Rosie started battling their
own demons, pulling away from him. "You two… you left me. All
alone."

Alexei walked over and clasped his neck. "I did. We both did.

But I swear to you, it wasn't because of you. We were in a bad place. I fought to come back from it, but Rosie wasn't strong enough. I'm sorry, man."

"Me too." Theo came in tight and hugged his long-lost brother.

"No one compares to Rosie but you still have me. I love you."

"Yeah, yeah." Theo pushed him away and wiped at his eyes with the back of his hand.

They removed stacks of pictures and paintings until the place was mostly clear. It felt… good. "How did she seem?" Theo couldn't stand to think about Reina upset.

"Ren? She's worried out of her mind. Kind of pissed, and right at the end, she cried because you called her a disappointment. But even then, the last thing she said to tell you was to stay safe. She thinks you're going to drive off a cliff."

"Shit! How do I fix this? We both have shit to work through." Theo sat on the couch, his head in his hands. "I yelled at her. I never yelled at Rosie once in my life."

"You're asking *me*? I'm the beauty; you're the brains, remember?" Alexei sighed. "Let's think about this for a minute. I suck at this, but Brynn tries to make me a better person all the time. She talks about being real. And honest."

"I'm real. I'm *too* real."

"Not with Rosie, you weren't. You put her so high on a pedestal, she couldn't see the ground. That's a hard thing to live up to."

"You saying I do that with Reina?"

"How the hell should I know? You tell me. I have enough trouble keeping track of my own woman."

"I'm lost."

"You yell at people. A lot. She's going to have to see that side of you eventually. If she can't take the real you, then she can't be with you. What else did she say?"

"It's hard to remember, but she talked about pleasing other people and putting them first. That she needed to learn how to say no, and she didn't want to hurt her ex's mom."

"Has she ever had trouble telling you no?"

"Never. And I told her that." Theo sat up. "She tells me no all the time. But she says it so nicely, I don't always realize what she's doing. She's sneaky like that." His foot tapped in agitation. "Sometimes, she drives me crazy and won't listen. When I asked her to check in with me the other day, she ignored me."

"That drives me crazy about Brynn, too. But you have to learn to trust her. Give her space." Alexei crossed his arms and leaned against the archway between rooms.

"When I wanted her to stop talking to Tío Hugo and give me some attention, she said no."

"Your tío is awesome. I'd rather talk to him, too." Alexei chuckled.

"He drives me crazy, too. The both of them." Theo scowled, but knew most people agreed with Alexei. "But I can't live without her. I don't want to."

"All this is good news. I think? You both need to be honest with each other. What else did you say to her?"

"I told her that I don't lie." Theo winced.

"You're an idiot." Alexei sat next to him on the couch. "Damn, Brynn must be rubbing off on me, because I've had another insight."

"What?"

"Did you tell her everything about Rosie? The drug use... everything?"

"No!" Theo fisted his hands, ready to punch his friend all over again. "I won't embarrass Rosie like that. She wouldn't want people to know." Theo's shoulders bunched. "I only told Reina she died in a fire."

"There you go. You *have* lied to her. You've got to tell her everything and listen to her when she tells you what's going on. Don't judge her. Not everyone is as perfect as you think you are." Alexei hit him upside the head—again.

"You better cut that shit out. And why does everyone keep telling me to listen?" He threw up his hands. "I get it! I get it! Don't hit me."

"Let's finish this up. For Rosie." He stood and offered Theo a hand up. "We'll do it right. Then we have a class to attend."

"The class. Reina is really worried about it." Theo grasped Alexei's hand and pulled himself up. "Do you think she'll forgive me, *acere?*"

"You're going to have to forgive yourself first. Rosie's choices were her own. Stop trying to control the world and appreciate what you have, right now."

Chapter 31

THIRD BASE

*B*ACK AT THE *scene of the crime.*

The charm school overflowed with people. Less than a week before, Ren had been walled in with polite introverts hoping to score a date. Now, she was surrounded by close to a hundred rowdy ladies, and quite a few men, ready to get down and dirty techniques about VJs.

From me.

A harrowing thirty minutes had flown by. Ren covered all of the requirements as far as sign-up sheets and the importance of safe sex—*plus* she hadn't collapsed from fear. Ready to tackle the big stuff, she flipped open the cunny book on a small podium in front of the room. Several friendly faces were scattered throughout the area. They offered support via inappropriate outbursts.

"Woo hoo!"

"Tell me how to make my *pusstache* sing."

"I believe in you, oral sex professional."

Ren smiled and discreetly placed her hand in her pocket. She grasped her rose quartz crystal, hoping it would keep her centered and open to love. Because she wished, with all her heart, that Theo would show up to the class.

"Thank you again for agreeing to spend the next few hours with me. Now that we've gotten through all the technical stuff. Let's get a little personal." Striving for her professional tone, the one that conveyed kindness and support, she continued, "I'll start with the ladies. How many of you enjoy—I mean *really* enjoy—oral sex?"

The room exploded. A few catcalls but also outright boos.

"I love it more than ice cream."

"*Meh*. Not for me."

"Does it have teeth?" A man with a knit cap asked, looking both terrified and intrigued.

Ren's mouth dropped open while the rest of the crowd cackled in glee.

"Oh, honey, if you have to ask that question, this is not the class for you," one of the women called out to him.

The man looked at his small group of friends, and they put their heads together for a mini powwow, eventually coming to a unanimous decision.

"We support the school, but we'll catch you at the next class, Ren." He saluted the crowd. "When the subject matter's a little more relevant to us."

All the regular attendees blew kisses and waved the men adieu.

Ren waved goodbye and focused back in on the demanding crowd, stumbling when the sheer number of people overwhelmed her. "Back to the original question." It was essential she gauge the mood of the room. She knew how complicated VJs could be for women, especially her. If it wasn't for Theo, she never—

Nope. Not going there.

"Did you guys notice the percentage of women that answered no? That they didn't care for VJs?" Ren studied the men who looked absolutely dumbfounded, as if they couldn't believe the negative response.

"That shows you how unique this whole process is. It's not as cut and dry as blowjobs. You'll be shocked to hear this, but women are *complicated*—and so are their vulvas. Not vaginas... *vulvas*. The vagina is the canal babies come out of." Ren smiled when a few of the men grumbled.

"Don't worry, we're going to cover the good, the bad, and the ugly of cunnilingus. We'll go over foreplay and interesting toys that can be used during the act." Ren briefly turned away when she felt her cheeks flame red, her words instantly reminding her of Theo and his vibrating tongue ring.

"Excuse me, dear. *Dear?*"

Ren turned toward the cheery voice. Thankfully, no one was looking at her full body flush. Instead, they were focused on a pink-haired octogenarian and a giant white board.

Uh-oh.

Ren searched for Brynn, who'd sworn she'd instructed Alexei to hide Ms. Scarlett's 3D vaginal diagram equipped with a glossary. My God, maybe that one *did* have teeth. It looked so...aggressive. When Ren finally spotted her friend, she saw not one, but *four* Calvo Quads. Brynn was surrounded by her sisters who were munching popcorn and cheering her on.

Unbelievable! Had this been a set up all along?

"Don't look at me like that," Brynn called out. "Yes. I was really on bedrest. And yes, I also knew my sisters *might* be back before the class began. But I wasn't sure." No one paid Brynn any attention because they were all staring at Ms. Scarlett. "You're doing great!"

Ren could only focus on one emergency at a time. Back to the rowdy crowd and...

"Dear. Oh, *dear.* I'm here. In the back. Can you see me?"

"Yes, Ms. Scarlett." Ren smiled, despite herself. "Do you have a question?"

"No, of course not. I'm an expert on the subject matter. I wanted to make sure everyone saw my chart and let them know I'm here for any additional instruction they may need." She tittered. "Not that you aren't doing a wonderful job. But I realized they might like a visual aid while you explained the process." She nodded and whipped the trifold from behind her back, holding it above her head so all could see.

As if they were one, a hundred heads looked up at the chart. Some gasped, many hooted and clapped, and quite a few groaned. Seeing the diagram of the female form, in all its specific glory, was even more startling under the ballroom lights.

Ren didn't know whether to laugh or cry. *The day she was having…* But instead of being mortified, well, she was a *little* mortified, Ren also felt…proud. Ms. Scarlett lived her life out loud. She never apologized, and Ren admired her for it. The Ladies should teach a class on having balls of steel.

"Thank you, Ms. Scarlett. As soon as I'm finished, I'll direct the rest of the questions to you."

"Oh, dear Lord, what is that man doing?" a woman shouted from the front row. The crowd was on their feet.

Ren scanned the room, cursing her short legs. She couldn't see anything.

"I can't unsee it."

"Good Lord!"

"Go, Boomer! Woo hoo!"

Ren's heart sank. *I've lost total control.* This class was an unmitigated disaster. Whatever was happening couldn't be good. "If everyone could please sit down, I'd be happy to elaborate on what—"

There was a break in the crowd, and Ren watched helplessly as Old Henry devoured a papaya that had been cut in half. He went to town as Ms. Scarlett clapped in delight, extremely pleased with her man.

"What is happening?" Ren called to Brynn, who had her hand over her mouth, tears running down her face.

Oh no. *Brynn is… laughing.* She was no help, at all. The rest of the Quads weren't much better. This was their school—shouldn't they be more upset? From what Ren could see, Athena shoveled popcorn in her mouth, Dacey hooted and slapped her leg, and Caelen…at least *she* had the decency to look scandalized.

Everything is falling apart!

Bam.

The charm school's doors flew open, and again, as one, everyone's heads swiveled toward the distraction—their attention briefly torn from Old Henry's attack on a poor defenseless papaya.

Ren's eyes went wide. She gazed at the mouthwatering sight, starting from the ground up as she took in thick-soled boots, jeans, and miles and miles of muscles. Two motorcycle gods stood before her, clouding the room in a haze of testosterone.

They dominated the space, but she only had eyes for Theo Romero. He looked so imposing with his bronze skin and hazel gaze. Somehow, the bruises made his impossibly pretty eyes look even greener.

So rugged. Devastatingly so.

The duo made their way up the aisle. Alexei took a hard left toward Brynn, but Theo kept coming. Straight ahead… toward her. A few of the women gasped, but most were groaning. Or maybe that was Ren, because nothing had ever looked so good.

When Theo made eye contact, his ferocious scowl firmly in place, she wasn't sure what it meant. He might kill her or kiss her. Either way, he couldn't do it *right now*, and he couldn't do it here. No matter how much she wanted him to.

Before Ren lost total control, she decided to head Theo off, to avoid a public argument. Clapping her hands twice, she said, "Thank you, Ms. Scarlett and Henry. Class, they'll be giving you a demonstration on some of the techniques we've gone over on a… papaya, that was totally planned, from day one." Ren raced down the aisle and met Theo halfway, trying to drag him back out the door.

"Reina." His deep voice vibrated through her, straight to her core. That impossibly bossy and demanding tone made her heart pound out of her chest.

"Are you okay?" She ran her eyes over his delicious body, fighting back a shiver as she studied him.

"I'm fine." He crossed his arms, not touching or hugging her like he usually did. "We need to talk."

"I can't talk right now." She tugged on him but he wasn't moving, so she whispered, "I'm teaching a class. Will you wait around until I'm finished?"

His scowl deepened. "I want to talk now."

Of course he did. She really needed to have a discussion with his mother about Theo's need for instant gratification.

"You can talk to him here, honey. We won't listen. Too much." A woman cackled and several people joined in.

Ren whipped around and looked at the expectant crowd. Unfortunately, no one seemed to be interested in Old Henry anymore. Even Ms. Scarlett had stopped watching.

"We want to know what's going on? Is that man planning to kill us? He looks deranged."

"What?" Ren eyed a conservatively dressed woman in the front row who she recognized immediately. She was a fixture at the charm school classes. "No, Mrs. Wong. Of course not. Theo and I had a bit of a misunderstanding, and I planned on speaking to him about it in private. After the class." She shot him a look, but he had his arms crossed, eyeing the crowd as if they had no right to interrupt *his* plans.

"No," Mrs. Wong said and pulled at the cuffs of her blazer. "I'm a paying customer. I demand to hear this conversation."

"No?" *What does that mean?* Ren looked at Brynn, who was wiping tears from under her eyes, tucked neatly against Alexei. "I don't have to listen to her, do I?"

"Yes, you do," someone yelled from the back of the class.

"Yeah, I want details. That's the best part of these classes."

"De-tails. De-tails. De-tails," the crowd chanted.

Ren would have agreed if she weren't the one in front of everyone.

"We will *not* be discussing our relationship in front of the class." Meanwhile, Theo had suddenly gone tight-lipped. Maybe she was too late? Maybe he did think she was a disappointment. "Why aren't you saying anything?" she whispered.

If possible, Theo's body tightened even further, but he still didn't answer, only continued to scowl at the class as if ready to pounce.

Maybe he was so upset that he couldn't vocalize the anger. *Well, then, I have nothing to lose.* "Fine. You want to talk? Let's talk. Come on." She dragged him back to the front of the class and sat him down in the front row. Right next to Mrs. Wong.

Chapter 32

TICKLE THE TEAPOT

THEO HATED BEING around all these greedy faces, desperate for information about his and Reina's lives. But when she'd asked why he hadn't spoken, his feelings were so jumbled, he hadn't known what to say. He'd insisted they speak because every minute they didn't, he felt her drifting away. Now she'd made him sit up front. But if his woman needed him here for moral support, he'd do it.

I'd do anything for her.

"You're not good enough for her." Mrs. Wong tilted her head toward Reina to emphasize her point.

"Agreed." He studied Reina. Everything about her was so vibrant, so special. Today, she wore a cream mini skirt and shirt with a mustard yellow blazer. Her usual scarf was missing, which gave him an unimpeded view of the beautiful vee of her cleavage. He shook off the X-rated images cascading through his mind and focused in on her words.

"I promised to *really* teach this class, even though I might have been set up." Reina gestured toward the Calvo Quads sitting in the back with Alexei.

Three of the four of them whooped it up while Brynn called,

"There was no set up. We nudged."

Reina squared her shoulders and faced the crowd. "I committed to this class, so that means I should be as vulnerable and open as you." She had her hand in her pocket and Theo would bet his bike she held one of her crystals.

"HELL YES."

"Finally! I was worried this class wouldn't be as good as the others."

"This is the *good* stuff I've been waiting for."

"Start at the beginning, girl. We want to hear *everything*."

Reina blushed and shook her head. "I won't start at the beginning. I'm sorry, Mrs. Wong. But *I will say* that both Theo and I have had issues because we've lost people we cared about." Ren brushed long bangs out of her eyes. "For me, those tough experiences have made me hesitant. When I get too close, I pull back, and I've disappointed Theo. He thinks I don't trust him."

"*Reina*." His chest felt tight, like he'd taken a hit to the solar plexus. "I don't—"

"Shh!" Mrs. Wong slapped his arm. "Don't interrupt."

"I want to show Theo I do trust him." Reina took a deep breath. "Earlier, there was a reason I asked how you felt about oral sex. I related to the women who looked uncomfortable. Maybe sharing a little of my own experience will help." Ren twined her fingers together.

Theo's heart dropped. His beautiful queen was going to go deep, and he wasn't sure these people had earned the right to hear her story. He cracked his knuckles and spun around in his seat, letting the guys know they better be respectful.

She licked her lips nervously and that fast, he was diamond hard.

Love those sexy lips.

"I had a bad experience with a man going...downtown." Reina's small smile fell. "I was convinced it wasn't for me because I couldn't climax from that kind of intimacy. My old partner made me feel self-conscious about it. He said… some damaging things. Even though a woman should *never* define herself by what others think about her, I avoided it like the plague."

"I'm so sorry." Ms. Hattie half rose in her chair, but one of The Ladies shushed her and sat her back down.

"We love you, Ren," Ai Zhao called from the back row, right by the door.

"You're so brave," Dacey yelled. "What happened next?"

Theo waited with clenched fists, monitoring the room to make sure no one hurt her feelings. But he had to admit, it seemed like a supportive group. *So far.* Right now, the guys looked like they wanted to melt away. Most were slumped in their seats or looking down at the ground.

Good. You don't deserve to look at her beauty.

"I didn't want to go into detail because there are a lot of men in this class, but you need to know that this might be an issue for some women—and if it is, be patient. And listen. Your partner may never be comfortable with it. Or she may need a little extra help with toys or other stimulation. Or she may love it. Either way, it's very personal and not something you should rush or demand. You also shouldn't feel upset if it doesn't work because it might not be about you."

That was going to be a blow for some of the guys, because pleasing your woman was a point of pride.

"So why's that dummy sitting up there? In the front row?" a woman asked, who sounded suspiciously like Viviana.

"I wanted to thank him and tell him he made me feel comforta-ble and… loved." Ren looked at him and reached out, as if she wanted to touch him, but wasn't sure. "I brought him up here so he knows how much I trust him. I wanted him to hear it in front of *everyone.* I never would've been able to teach the class without him."

Theo's chest felt warm, Reina's words a calming balm. He

fought to remain composed. This moment was private and he would only share it with Reina.

"But he's still not smiling. Look! He's frowning at you."

"No, I'm not." *My face just looks like that.* Theo glowered at the room.

"People assume that when they don't know him. I think Theo Romero looks deliciously scary." She smiled, unfazed by the comments.

I may be obsessed with this woman.

"Delicious? With those black eyes?"

"Yes." Ren laughed softly. "He's tough, with a big ole chip on his shoulder, but if he cares about you...he puts you first. I hope you're all lucky enough to find someone who'll do that for you."

"You're in love, chica. Admit it!"

"W-what?" Ren's cheeks blazed bright red, splotches appearing on her neck and face. "We haven't known each other that long. We can't use the L word yet. That's crazy! Not that I should have said 'yet'. Who knows if he ever will? *Omigod.*" Her hands fluttered around, clearly upset. "I wanted you to know that I feel comfortable being myself around him. He never shuts me up because I talk *a lot.* He's patient with my insecurities... and he's so smart! When he talks math, I have no idea what he's saying, but it's super sexy."

"Math is *not* sexy. You've got it bad, girl."

"I do." She sighed and looked over at him. "But I wasn't quite ready to admit it to myself."

"But what about *him*? Does he feel the same way?"

"I don't know. I can't speak for him." Ren waved off the question. "It's not fair to ask him in front of everyone. This moment is about me, sharing *my* feelings. Besides, we need to get back to the class. I'm sorry for the sidetrack." Reina turned and refused to look at him. Her shoulders were tight and her smile strained.

Aww, hell no. Theo relived every emotion, every excruciating second he'd waited for her to call him. Six long months he'd done nothing but imagine her smile—even before she'd spoken a word to him. He stood. "You know, Reina," he rumbled out past tight lips, hating to say this in front of everyone but needing her to know.

"Know what?" Her gaze snapped up to his.

"It doesn't matter that it's only been a few days—you *know* how I feel about you." He rubbed his hands on his thighs, desperate to touch her.

"Even after earlier today?" she whispered.

"What happened earlier today?"

Theo's gaze shot over to the man who dared to interrupt while he spoke to his girl. He wilted as Theo stared him down.

"Y-you love me?" Reina touched his arm.

"I do." He cupped her cheek. "I thought about you constantly, waited for you to choose me." He cleared his throat, the tender words stuck in his throat. "When we finally spoke... I knew you were the one for me."

"I love you, too." Ren threw her arms around his neck.

"They're in love!" Ms. Hattie cried and jumped up. The room devolved into chaos, people shouting and high-fiving each other. Theo remained focused on his prize. His Reina loved him. Life didn't get better than this.

Chapter 33

TRUE LOVE'S KISS

"WE DID IT." Ren cuddled up on Theo's lap. They ended up in Ms. Belle's backyard, a sprawling expanse that covered a large cul-de-sac. The covered bench they found, tucked back toward the back of the school, gave them a front row view to rolling hills, twinkling lights, and colorful hydrangeas. It reminded Ren of a fairy garden she'd visited as a child.

It was well past midnight. The congratulations, and eventually the actual class instruction, had taken hours. But now, the last of the guests were gone. Alexei had taken Brynn home, The Ladies were snuggled up in bed, and no one else was staying overnight in the quiet school. After all the insanity, with people *and* papaya, they had the place to themselves.

Ren took a deep breath, relieved to be in his arms but ready to broach some of their issues. "I hate it when we fight. I thought I'd pushed you away. I can't… I don't know how to compete with your memories of the past. I wasn't sure if you'd show up tonight."

"I'll never give up on you, Reina. It would hurt too much."

His words melted away some of her worry and insecurities.

"I loved what you said." The side of his mouth kicked up. "But I never want to talk about my feelings in front of that many people again."

She giggled and nodded. "Agreed."

He let out a deep breath and looked up at the night sky. "Alexei and I cleaned out Rosie's stuff. It's gone."

"How do you feel about that?" She ran her hands down his arms, shocked at the raw words. But that was Theo, blunt and to the point.

"Good, I think. We gave most of it to her mom. All her things had been there so long, I almost didn't see it anymore. Which made me feel worse when you brought it up." He sighed. "I didn't want to throw her away."

He might be the sweetest man on the planet, and maybe she needed to remind herself he wasn't as tough as he seemed. "I'm so sorry. I handled the whole thing the wrong way. I don't get mad often, but when I do, I don't think through what I'm trying to say."

"Get used to it."

"Being mad at you?"

"Yeah, I've been told I'm a handful by…everybody." He brushed his cheek against hers. "I'm not going to say sorry for yelling at you because apparently that's a part of who I am. I need you to know that's how I express myself. I don't want you to be afraid of me."

She laughed out loud. "I've never been afraid of you."

"I know. I love that about you." Theo's leg tapped a constant beat, jostling her as they spoke. "One more thing, I was full of shit when I said I never lied to you."

Her hands stilled on his chest. "You lied to me?"

"The first lie was blatant. You've never been a disappointment to me. *Never.*" He let out a deep breath. "Do you believe me?"

"Yes." They'd both said stupid things in the heat of the moment.

"The second was through omission. I didn't tell you the whole story about Rosie and why I get so tied up about it."

"You can tell me anything." She pressed a soft kiss against his lips.

Theo squeezed his eyes shut. "I *hate* to talk about this." He took a deep breath. "She was… a drug addict."

Ren ran her hands over his shoulders, his back, wherever she could reach, to show she cared. He could take as long as he needed to get it out.

"Both Rosie and Alexei struggled with addiction. I tried and tried to bring them back. It gutted me because…it felt like they were abandoning me. The two closest people in the world chose drugs over me." He thumped his fist against his chest. "I couldn't admit I was mad at Rosie, so I directed it all at Alexei. He almost died in the same fire that took her life. For years, I wanted to kill him. I was so pissed. I thought he'd taken her there, but it turned out I had it all wrong. We talked it out, and I helped get him out of *la mafia*." He pressed the heels of his palms against his eyes. "*Coño*, I hate this but…that's the important parts. I wanted you to know."

"I understand. Addiction is a terrible disease. When you're ready, you can tell me about Rosie." She adjusted herself to get closer. "So you don't feel like you're forgetting her. And I can take you to see Nicholas. H-his mom is dying."

"Is that why you were pulling away?" He shook his head. "What do I have to do to get you to count on me? I'm here for you!"

"Don't get loud. I know. You're right." She sighed. "I'm working on it, I swear. But I've been alone a long time. I don't have many friends. I only reconnected with the Calvo Quads when they started teaching the classes. I'd shut myself off from hurt because I lost most of the people I loved in a short amount of time."

"I'm sorry."

"I know. But it means you'll have to be patient with me." She ran her fingers through his hair. "Theo, I'm a package deal. Nicholas was always going to be a part of my life, but now that his mom is sick, I'll be handling his affairs. It's what she wants." She cocked her head to the side, to study his reaction. "How do you feel about that?"

"I have no choice. Whatever you decide, I want to do it together." He cleared his throat. "One last thing, and I'm done with talking about all this shit." His hands banded around her like he never wanted to let go. "I have an email I want to open with you."

"You do? What is it?" She waited as he pulled out his phone.

"It's my acceptance or rejection letter from USC. I brought it with me the night I came over to your place."

"The day you couldn't reach me? Oh my God, you wanted to share this with me, and I did that to you? I'm so sorry."

"I know." He kissed her within an inch of her life. "Before I open it, I want you to know—I'm done with *la mafia*. Permanently. But I'm still going to ride my bike."

"But only on your birthday?" She sighed when he frowned again. "Maybe just holidays or special occasions? No?"

"*Reina*. I have to ride. It's a part of me." His frown eased. "But I promise not to take off when we get in a fight."

She nodded. He loved his bike. She'd have to grin and bear it. "Okay, I agree. Open the email. I can't wait!"

He closed his eyes briefly and then focused on the phone, swiping it with his finger.

The text was too small for her to read. "What does it say?"

"It's talking about academic probation because of what happened before but... I'm in!"

"You did it!" She threw her arms around his shoulders, holding on for dear life as he popped up and ran through the yard, pumping his fist in the air. "I'm so proud of you." She hooked her legs around his waist.

Hefting her until she felt the bulge of his raging erection, he kissed her and ran his big hands up her thighs.

She moaned and undulated against him, his hard cock rubbing her right where she needed it.

"You're so beautiful, Reina. I need you."

"Here?" she asked without her usual hesitation. She wanted it too, needed him so badly after the uncertainty of the day. "Do you want to go inside?"

"You tell me." He thrust against her—making her clench with need. "Here, or inside?"

"Here, *please*." He went back to their nook at the back of the yard, in their own magical world. She didn't want to be anywhere else. She ran her lips down his neck, biting and licking his thick muscles.

He fell back against the cushioned bench while she stood, shucking her tights and panties. When she straddled him again, her skirt fluttered around them, giving them an added bit of privacy.

Theo moaned, plunging a finger inside of her. "So wet. For me."

"I always am. The minute I see you. I want you," she whispered.

"Unbutton my pants, Reina."

She slid back on his lap and undid the buttons, one by one. Anticipation made her breasts pebble. "Shoot."

"What?" He grunted when his large cock popped free, bouncing against his abs.

"I wanted to give you a blowjob. I learned so much from Caelen's class. But this feels so good." She squeezed her thighs and rode over the length of him, coating his cock in her dripping lips, pausing at the tip but never impaling him.

"Yes! Keep doing that." He grasped her hips and tipped her pelvis forward and back to skim his rock-hard member. "No blowjob. Can't take it. This feels perfect." He pulled her shirt and bra above her chest and suckled her breast.

"Yes!" She hissed, trying to keep it down. All she could feel was the cool air on her wet nipples and Theo's warm tongue. Best feeling *ever*. "But I want to take you in my mouth. I want to lick your balls and run my tongue over your mushroom head."

"You *what?*" He groaned. "What happened to the shy girl who read a manual while I went down on her?"

"You created a monster. All I can think about is sucking your rock...hard..." she pushed her boobs together because she knew it drove him crazy, "cock, coasting over my tongue. It would feel *so good.*"

"Those words are... *killing* me." His face tightened. "Reach into my jeans and put the condom on."

"But I want to try."

"Can't stop thinking about it, but I'm too far gone. Need inside of you *now.*"

She found the condom, fumbled with the wrapper, and rolled it down him.

He angled his cock right at her entrance. "Touch yourself."

She reached between them, her silky lips glazing her fingers.

He held himself there, teasing her with his tip.

"Deeper, Theo!"

"No." He clenched his jaw. "Want to see how much you want me."

Driven to distraction, she thrust against him, trying to impale herself on him. She watched his expressive face while he stared in fascination at his head bumping her lips. *Time to drive him crazy.* She grabbed her aching breasts and licked the tip of her nipples.

He roared in response, plunging inside of her.

"Yes. Thank you, *thank you,*" she chanted against his neck to muffle her cries. She rode him hard, snapping her hips to chase her orgasm.

He devoured her breasts, ramming into her like a piston.

Clutching his head to her chest, she whispered, "Now, now. It's *now.*" Spasming over his thick length, she felt her core contracting around him. Pleasure slammed up her spine. The intensity continued through her limbs, making her toes curl.

"Can't stop. Feels so good." He pounded inside of her, thrusting his hips, flinging back his head and opened his lips to—

She slapped a hand over his mouth to muffle the roar, her body quaking as he squeezed her thighs, bucking against her one last time. She collapsed against him, their uneven breathing the only thing she could process as his chest rose and fell.

She was a boneless mess, all of the tension of the past day evaporating like steam.

After a few beautiful minutes, Theo whispered, "I love you, Reina. Tell me you'll put up with me, and give me a shot. Even with my ugly mug frowning all the time. I've waited six months for you. Tell me it's been worth it."

She pulled up from his chest and cupped his cheeks, loving the rough feel of his beard on her sensitive palms. "I love you. Which means you're stuck with me. Warts and all."

He held her tight until their hearts slowed and the night became uncomfortably cool. He stood with her in his arms and walked her to the back door of the charm school.

"I'm so glad you kept all those guys away from me at speed dating." She sighed and laid her head against his chest. "That's when I think I knew I couldn't live without the bossy Theo Romero, even though everybody else thought I should be furious."

"I knew the minute you said we should make-out to ease the tension that you were the one for me." He kissed her lips and walked her through the door. "Nothing I like better than kissing my Reina."

(Turn the page for a sneak peek of what's coming next!)

COMING SOON:
Charm School Role Play: Lesson 7

INTERESTED IN WHERE IT ALL BEGAN?

Caelen Calvo and her sisters inherit a bankrupt charm school. To keep the doors open, Caelen decides to teach very *adult*, and very *naughty* classes. Each sister is in charge of her own class, and has to bone-up on subject matter like: mouth hugs, toys, sensation play and more…

The only problem? None of them are currently in relationships. So they're going to have to get creative, and find sexy guinea pigs to help them research the class.

Read Caelen and Dare's story for book 1 in the Charm School Series.

Charm School After Dark: Book 1

Other Books by Lynn Garcia Carmer

Contemporary Romance

Charm School After Dark: Lesson 1 (Charm School Series)

Charm School Quickie: Lesson 1.5 (Charm School Series)

Charm School All-Nighter: Lesson 2 (Charm School Series)

Charm School Night Play: Lesson 3 (Charm School Series)

Charm School Billionaire Bad Boy: Lesson 4 (Charm School Series)

Charm School Christmas Karma: A Steamy Holiday Romance (Charm School Series)

Charm School Lip Service: Lesson 6 (Charm School Series)

Just For Tonight (Victoria Bay Series) Book 1

Just Don't Go (Victoria Bay Series) Book 2

Paranormal/Sci-Fi Romance

The Lasting (Gargoyle Legend) Book 1

Fervor (The Fervor Chronicles) Book 1

Note from the Author

I love Ren and Theo! The grumpy Cuban has been a favorite, and it was a relief to finally get their story down. Ren, aka Reina, aka Adrenilda popped on the pages in book 2 of the charm school series: *Charm School All-Nighter: Lesson 2.*

I knew from page one that Ren had Alopecia Areata. I researched the disease and joined a support group on FB where women and men were open and vulnerable about their struggles and triumphs with the disease. I want to thank them from the bottom of my heart.

I love this series, and I don't want it to be the end. Don't you worry, Blue and Aitana will get their story. Thank you for the support, and please consider writing an honest review.

Besitos,
Lynn

CONTACT ME

If you'd like to sign up for my newsletter, to learn the latest on the Calvo Quads and the hunky heroes that love them—or maybe you just want to drop a line and say hello on social media, please contact me at:

Lynncarmerauthor.com
Facebook Reader's Group: @Carmer's Charmers
FB Author Page: Lynn Garcia Carmer Author
Tik Tok: @Lynngarciacarmer
Twitter: @Lynncarmer
Instagram: @Lynngarciacarmer
Email: Lynncarmer@ymail.com

ACKNOWLEDGEMENTS

I want to thank Emily Gray and Eliza March for helping me plot this book—you guys are the best! Big thanks to Keara for her unending support.

Last but not least, thank you to my hunky husband for letting me, be me.

ABOUT THE AUTHOR

Amazon Bestselling Author Lynn Garcia Carmer is a talker, a writer, a reader, a teacher, a procrastinator, an avid fan of all show's reality, and a "devourer" of all thing's sweet. She is having the *best* time working on red-hot and humorous, multicultural, sci/fi, paranormal, and contemporary romance novels.

Here's to hunky heroes and hot-blooded heroines!

www.ingramcontent.com/pod-product-compliance
Lightning Source LLC
Chambersburg PA
CBHW060917180626
46817CB00004B/1302